Khalid Al Hajeri is an Emirati author living in the United Arab Emirates. He graduated with a Bachelor of Arts degree in English Language and Literature in the year 2008, and is an avid collector and reader of books on various fiction and non-fiction topics. *The Third One* is his first novel.

To my mother, who gave me everything and was always by my side through and through. Words alone cannot describe how much I love her for all that she has done for me in my life.

Khalid Al Hajeri

THE THIRD ONE

AUSTIN MACAULEY PUBLISHERS™
LONDON • CAMBRIDGE • NEW YORK • SHARJAH

Copyright © **Khalid Al Hajeri 2023**

The right of Khalid Al Hajeri to be identified as author of this work has been asserted by the author in accordance with Federal Law No. (7) of UAE, Year 2002, Concerning Copyrights and Neighboring Rights.

All rights reserved. No part of this publication may be reproduced, stored in a retrieval system, or transmitted in any form or by any means, electronic, mechanical, photocopying, recording, or otherwise, without the prior permission of the publishers.

Any person who commits any unauthorized act in relation to this publication may be liable to legal prosecution and civil claims for damages.

This is a work of fiction. Names, characters, businesses, places, events, locales, and incidents are either the products of the author's imagination or used in a fictitious manner. Any resemblance to actual persons, living or dead, or actual events is purely coincidental.

The age group that matches the content of the books has been classified according to the age classification system issued by the Ministry of Culture and Youth.

ISBN – 9789948785248 – (Paperback)
ISBN – 9789948785255 – (E-Book)

Application Number: MC-10-01-6645240
Age Classification: 17+

Printer Name: iPrint Global Ltd
Printer Address: Witchford, England

First Published 2023
AUSTIN MACAULEY PUBLISHERS FZE
Sharjah Publishing City
P.O Box [519201]
Sharjah, UAE
www.austinmacauley.ae
+971 655 95 202

Special thanks goes to Austin Macauley Publishers for helping me realize my dream of publishing my first novel.

Prologue

Searching. That's what I've been doing so far: Searching. I do not know when I will find it, but I know that I will find it very soon.

And what is *it* that I am searching for, you may ask? I'm afraid *it* is difficult to explain at this moment in time. Earlier, I was driving on a long stretch of highway searching for that special thing. *It* is something that will mean a lot to me, so much so that I cannot explain what *it* is right now. I was driving on the semi-deserted highway, searching searching, searching...

For *it*.

Perhaps now is the time to stop rambling about my search. I take back what I said about the difficulty in explaining my search to you. I had pulled over to the side of the road, switched off the engine of my car, and stepped out to stretch my legs and walked into a sandy wasteland that humanity proudly defines as a 'desert'. A little shack rested not far from the road, between two overgrown desert bushes. I had entered this shack, closing the door behind me to sit in near darkness. The only light I saw was the bright moonlight viewed from a small crack in the wooden wall. But then I flipped the switch to turn on the little lamp in the corner, in order to write down my story.

Since I had reached my destination, I was able to think more clearly about everything. I will finally explain what had happened to me before and what made me motivated to search for *it*.

Before I begin my story, I'd like to tell you that my name was Omar. My old name.

Completion

I had just finished my university studies and graduated with a bachelor's degree in English, with the highest honors. My friends and family celebrated my graduation with me with great happiness, and I was the happiest out of all of them. After six whole years, I finally managed to prove to everyone that I was able to take on the world of higher learning. I felt very proud of myself, and my father even more so.

"My son can take on the world now, get a good job, and raise a family!" said my overconfident father to my family members in the living room. I felt slightly embarrassed after he said that, but I just stood there and flashed a smile while he patted me on the back. My two young cousins giggled and Jasem, the younger of the two, asked me in a mischievous manner, "Since you finished university, will you work for me?" Everyone in the room burst out in laughter, and I saw Jasem's right ear being pulled playfully by his mother. "Hey now, don't make fun of Omar. He will definitely find a great place to work," Jasem's mother beamed. After that, everyone chatted with each other, and I sat down on the sofa relishing this amazing moment I was in, a time when every single person from my family was willing to spend time with each other for the sake of my graduation from university.

After the celebration, the days passed my quickly. I found myself applying for jobs online, with the websites offering many fields to work in relation to the area that I studied. It was kind of fun to browse for jobs online; I felt more in control of my choices and for the first time, used the internet in a grown-up way, rather than for student research and for playing online video games.

Then months passed; I was still at home without a job. Concerned about my own situation, I asked my parents if it was a good idea to physically visit possible places to work at, instead of being at home and waiting for phone calls or emails from the places I applied for online. My father said nothing, but my mother asked me, "Did any of your friends get a place to work after they graduated?"

I told her, "Yes, almost all of them did."

Then she told me, "Try going directly to the companies and hand in your CVs yourself, maybe you will have more luck." I nodded and told her I would try her advice.

Before I left the room, my mother added, "Don't worry too much about finding a job. It took your father an entire *year* to finally get a place to work!" She laughed aloud, but my father frowned and did not say anything. I walked out of the room, grabbed my car key, and started driving away from my house, ready to personally give my CVs to companies in the hope of getting hired for a decent job.

But while driving, I thought about my father. I thought about his unusual silence throughout the conversation. He seemed to be upset with something, probably the fact that I did not start working yet even months after my graduation from university. I prayed that he would have faith in me trying my best to find work.

And I *did* get a job eventually. Something unusual that would change my life forever, and no going back.

Friend

I first stopped to fuel up my car at a rather neglected petrol station. Feeling rather thirsty and a little hungry, I decided to buy a bottle of water and a bag of potato chips while I was there. I fueled up the car and then proceeded to the mini-mart located on the side of the petrol pump. Save for myself and a lady at the cashier counter, there was no one else in the mini-mart. I grabbed the water and chips from the food section and casually walked around the isles when I remembered that it was my younger sister Noora's birthday tomorrow. So I looked around in the toy section and found a surprising variety of toys.

I had a look at a collection of dolls, and my eyes were fixed on a small red-haired female doll wearing a red flower dress and a red ribbon around its neck. The eyes were a cyan blue, and the cheeks had round pink blush marks that were painted on each side. It looked cute enough for Noora to have in her doll collection.

I returned to the cashier to purchase the food and drink and the doll, and to pay for the petrol. She smiled, placed my purchases in an unmarked black plastic bag, and then I took the bag and walked outside to my car. I set the bag of things I bought on the passenger seat, and drove away from the petrol station.

Before starting my journey going to companies to give them my CVs in the hopes of getting hired for a job, I made a decision to stop by a friend's house to let him know what I was doing that day. That friend of mine is named Mark.

Mark was 23 years old (the same age as I was at the time), graduated, and still did not find a job. Aside from the fact that I did not find a job either, the only differences between us were that the university degrees we earned were of different fields, and that he was a lazy guy compared to me. He graduated with a degree in computer science, and he did not even start looking for a job. He was always busy playing his video games at home, taking advantage of his father being gone on business trips and his mother working in an office far from home. I frequently advised him to take a break from his video gaming hobby, but he never really listened to my words.

Nevertheless, I felt it was good to pay Mark a visit once in a while, and today was the day to do so since the first company I wanted to apply to in person was only a few blocks away from his house. After arriving to the parking space located in front of Mark's villa, I exited the car and walked over to the front door of his house.

I pushed the button of the doorbell, but suddenly I remembered that his bell did not work for more than three years, due to his being too lazy to call technicians to repair it, despite me reminding him time and time again. So I pulled out my cell phone from my pocket and dialed his number to call him. "Hello…Omar?" a groggy voice answered. It was Mark, it sounded like he had just woken up from sleep.

"Hey, Mark, I hope you're doing all right. I am outside your house at the moment, just wanted to visit. Is it all right if I come in?" There was a short pause, then he told me it was fine. Then he hung up, and sure enough, Mark opened the door for me and welcomed me to come inside.

"What's up Omar? How are ya doin' today?" he asked me hurriedly.

I told him, "Just came for a visit before I go job hunting." He led me to his room, sat down on his gaming chair, and I sat down next to him on the sofa. Not surprisingly, he picked up his video game controller and continued playing his first-person shooter game. I said to him for the thousandth time, "You should take a break from your gaming hobby and start looking for a job, Mark. We all need to try looking for work and move on with our adult lives." After I said that, he violently threw his controller to the ground, smashing a half-empty soft drink glass bottle to smithereens which created a fizzy green mess on his white carpet.

"Can you, like, stop telling me this every day you see me?" he screamed. I was actually shocked by his reaction; he never reacted like this before. He normally used to say, "Yeah, yeah, I'll do that another day." But today, something was definitely wrong with him.

I carefully asked Mark, "Why did you get so angry? You never got mad at me when I said it to you before."

Tearfully, after a few long seconds, he replied, "I...I don't know, man. I don't know why...I got mad so fast." Then I told him, "Don't worry about it; I'll leave you alone now. I have to go and submit CVs today."

So he showed me to the door, we bid farewell to each other, and I exited his home. As I walked to the target company to give in my CV, I thought about both my father's and Mark's strange reactions. Much later on, I would find out that the reason to their strangely negative mood swings was due to something out of the ordinary.

Vanished

I decided to go back to my car and drink some water that I had bought from the petrol station earlier. After the out-of-nowhere outburst I witnessed from Mark at his house, I felt I needed to quench my thirst and free my mind from bothersome thoughts popping into my head.

As I unlocked the doors of my car and opened the driver's side door, I noticed something strange. The bag of things I had purchased looked smaller than before. I quickly grabbed the black plastic bag and emptied the contents on the driver's seat. Out fell the bag of potato chips, the bottle of water, and...

I did not see the doll fall out of the bag, nor did I see it *in* the bag.

The doll was gone.

Did I possibly leave it behind at that old petrol station? I could have sworn that the cashier put it in the bag with the rest of the things I had bought. I quickly decided to return to the petrol station and see if the cashier forgot to stuff the doll in the bag.

When I arrived at the station, I walked into the mart as calmly as I could, and asked the cashier about the doll. She insisted that she *did* put it in the bag, and she proved this to me by showing me footage on the security camera. The video recording showed that she had indeed placed the doll inside the bag.

Feeling defeated, I thanked the cashier for her help and drove away from the petrol station. I gave some more thought into the mysterious disappearance of the doll that was supposed to be my young sister's birthday present. Was it possible that I had left the doll at Mark's house? No, that was not possible, since I did not carry the bag into his house to begin with. But of course I *did* buy the doll. After all, I still have the receipt which proves that I had bought it. So I asked myself in my mind, what in the world happened to it?

I could not answer that question. I honestly had no idea what happened to it. Perhaps it was time for me to go home now, since I was not in the mood to go to any company to give in my CVs anymore. I promised myself to go to the companies tomorrow, so I can relax at home for the rest of the day and then think about the vanishing of the doll.

I finally reached home and pulled into the driveway of my house. After switching off the engine, I noticed that the gate of my house was left open and that both my parents' cars were gone. I guessed they must have forgotten to close the gate after leaving…but that was unusual. Even more strange was the fact that when I entered the house there was no sign of my sister Noora. Perhaps she had gone with her friends somewhere, I thought.

I washed my face in the kitchen, then walked down the hallway to my room and entered inside. My jaw dropped when I glanced at my perfectly made-up bed.

The doll was sitting in the exact middle of my bed, lying on its back, seemingly greeting me with its innocently fixed smile. I slowly walked to the bed and picked up the doll with my hands. I laughed hysterically for almost thirty seconds, my hands squeezing the soft plushy material of the doll. Suddenly, I felt a sharp pain jolting in my right hand, and I cried out as I threw the doll onto the floor. Cradling my hurt right hand with my other, I lifted my foot above the doll in an angry attempt to stomp on it. But when I looked down…

The doll was gone…again.

Maybe I threw it down so hard that it rolled under my bed. I kneeled down to look underneath, and it wasn't there. Where did it go? And more importantly, why did I feel pain in my hand when I squeezed it? Surely, I was squeezing something made of soft plush, but it felt like squeezing the razor-sharp thorns of a porcupine!

Normally, if a another person was in my place, he/she would go get him/herself checked into a psychiatric ward after seeing what I had seen and feeling what I had felt. I tried calming myself down by drinking a half-filled bottle of water that was sitting on the computer desk in my room. Perhaps this is a dream, I thought to myself. I probably just need to lie in bed and make the dream normal again. So I lay in bed and closed my eyes, waiting for my overly active brain to shut off in order to forget this crazy dream and wake up into a dreamless reality.

I woke up when I heard my mobile phone ringing in my pocket. I answered the call. It was my mother. "Your father wants to tell you something. He's in the living room," she said to me in a soft troubled voice, and then she abruptly dropped the call. After she hung up, I glanced at the clock on my dresser. It was ten o'clock in the morning. I apparently overslept; that dream I had yesterday was so weird and intense that I must have felt very exhausted during my sleep.

Forgetting about my dream, I got out of bed, still dressed in my clothing from yesterday, and walked towards the living room to see what the fuss was about. My dad was sitting on his favorite chair watching a soccer match on television.

As soon as he looked up at me, he got up from the chair, switched off the television, and grabbed me by the chest and pushed me against the wall. "Today…tomorrow…and the days after that…I don't want to see you in the house until the sun sets," he said to me slowly but aggressively. His eyes were blood red, and his face looked flushed with a furious expression. A few seconds after he said that, he let go of me but still maintained his red-eyed stare towards me.

He continued, "I am very disappointed in you, Omar. It has been months, and you still didn't find a place to work. I knew you shouldn't have studied English in university; if you had studied Chemical Engineering like I did, you would have been accepted into a job in the very first week after your graduation." I was so stunned that I did not know how to respond to what he was saying, so I kept silent and let him talk more. "I want you to go out and find a job by yourself, but come back home by night. I will not help you because I want to show you how it feels to try finding a job by yourself. Your mother knows nothing about job-hunting; *I* was the one who got her the job at the bank! So go out and look for a job, and don't come back until tonight."

After that tense speech my dad had given me, I obediently walked to my room, changed my clothes, gathered my wallet and car key and suitcase containing my CVs and documents, and hurriedly drove away from home. I still felt like I was in the dream, since my father acted very abnormal to the point that I did not really recognize him. I did not know whether I was dreaming or not, but I was motivated to get as far away from my house as possible. And afterwards, I would find myself being gone from home for longer than just a day. I did not return, in fact.

The Company

I remembered the promise I made to myself yesterday to visit the company located near Mark's house. Luckily, there was plenty of parking available – in fact, the whole parking lot behind the company building was empty save for a beat-up gray-colored van parked in a handicap parking space. As I stepped out of my car, which I had parked close to the building, I curiously approached the odd-looking van. I noticed that the van had no license plate, nor did it have a handicap sticker anywhere on it. The guy driving this thing will definitely be fined by the police and the vehicle impounded, I thought to myself.

The automatic front door slid open as I approached, and I entered into the reception area. The reception room was practically as blank as the parking lot; only the reception desk was in this room, completely without any waiting chairs. I advanced to the desk, ready to hand in my CV to the blonde female receptionist.

As I took one final step closer to the desk, the receptionist looked up and a smile beamed on her face. "Ah yes, Omar! The manager has been expecting you," she proclaimed happily in English in her British accent.

Confused, I replied to her, "I was being expected? There must be a mistake; I just arrived here to hand in my CV. I never visited your company before and don't know anybody here."

She paused for a second, and then she said, "No, this is no mistake! Our company has been observing you for some time now, and the manager stated that he saw potential in you." She handed me a red slip of blank paper, then said, "This is your security pass; take it with you up to the third floor. Good luck!"

Admittedly dumbfounded, I followed her instructions and stepped into the open elevator on the left side of the counter to go to the third floor and meet the manager of this company. The receptionist smiled and waved as the elevator doors closed...

*****

Before I continue my story further, I am sure you are asking yourself, 'Why isn't Omar mentioning the company's name?' Here is a simple answer from me to you: This company did not really have a name. The truth is, the company did have a name the last time I found out about it through the internet, but later on its name changed to something else. Its name constantly changed throughout my story, so after I reveal one of its names to you, I will not bother to list any more of its infinite numbers of names. However, just keep in mind that this company is extraordinary, and therefore it does not follow the standardized laws of business in our current world.

Now I shall continue with my story...

*****

Once the elevator reached the third floor, I waited for the doors to open, and then exited the elevator slowly. All of a sudden, I stood dead still, in front of the closed doors of the elevator, trying to take in what I was seeing.

This part of the building was much different from its bland exterior and ground floor reception room. Flowering and non-flowering plants of many kinds were in golden pots that sat in front of aqua-colored walls. Various paintings featuring people and lush landscapes hung on the parts of the walls that were not occupied by the plants. The floor looked like it was made of exquisite white marble which slightly reflected the bright yellow lights above me. I looked up and saw that the lights on the flawless ceiling rested on mini chandeliers made of diamond crystals.

The beautiful scenery of this third-floor lobby gripped my senses for more than a minute. After I regained control of myself, I forced my legs to carry me towards the only door that I could see in the room. The word 'manager' was capitalized, labeled in vivid white ink on a black background card, on the fine, black-painted wooden door. I knocked three times, and heard a booming voice call out, "Come in, Omar." Startled, I reached for the shiny silver knob, pressed it downwards, and then pushed open the door.

Surprisingly, the manager's room looked very simplistic compared to the splendid room which I was in earlier. I saw a pot of roses sitting on a small table near a window, one painting of a gray battleship hanging above a little bookshelf, and a coffee table with a small statue of a whale sitting in the center. The walls, the ceiling, and the floor of the room were gray color. The manager's desk and chair, and the guest chair, were colored a basic black. The manager himself wore an old-fashioned black suit, but without a tie.

"Welcome, Omar. Please sit down," the bald-headed manager ordered politely in an American accent, motioning with his right hand to the guest chair. I sat down, and noticed one more piece of furniture: a coat hanger holding a black leather trench coat and a gray leather fedora hat.

"So tell me, Omar, do you know why you are here?" the manager asked.

I replied quickly, "To find a place to work." Suddenly, the manager laughed a laughter sounding like a fusion of coughing and chuckling. I noticed that the manager's face was extremely pale, almost a ghostly transparent crystal white.

After he stopped laughing, he said to me, "I already assigned you a job!"

I was surprised at what he told me at that moment. I was expecting an on-the-spot interview with the manager or something similar, but this…this was too weird to be actually happening. I did not know for sure if I was dreaming or not.

"Ever since you entered that gas station, I, along with my associates, have been monitoring you. We saw that you didn't mind driving into a low-classed gas station, didn't care that it looked too cheap for you." He paused to sneeze and excused himself, then continued, "You were also willing to buy a few things from the mini mart of the gas station, even though the mart was just as low-classed as its gas station. Face it, kid, even the potato chips you bought from the mart were practically rubbish…"

He stopped his words short, and laughed in that cough-chuckle laughter again. "Actually, one of the things you bought from the place was definitely not rubbish. The doll you bought…she's worth something." The manager sneezed and excused himself again. Then he continued, "She is one of our employees; we put her out there to test an unsuspecting person who would buy her. She tested you from the moment you handed the money to the cashier to buy her."

My eyes widened. *This has got to be a dream,* I thought. There was no way in real life that a manager would refer to a doll as an employee of his company. What is going on here?

Again, as if he had heard my thoughts, he said to me, "And by the way, Omar, if you're thinking this is a dream, you're wrong. This is real. Go ahead; try pinching yourself to wake up from this 'dream.' Or better yet, let me pour this on you." He hit his right fist hard onto his desk, and I felt water gushing onto my head from the ceiling. The water was ice cold.

I involuntarily cried out and jumped up from my seat, already shivering from the feeling of the freezing water soaking in my hair. I looked up and saw that the ceiling had a tile that opened sideways, and I saw a hole in the opening which was where the water gushed from. I assumed the manager had slammed his fist on a concealed button on his desk, which opened the ceiling tile above me and let water spill on me, just like in a movie or in a cartoon show. So I wasn't dreaming after all, I thought. If I had been dreaming, then at this very moment the manager and his room would have vanished, and I would have found myself awake in my own room at my house, with cold sweat on my face instead of cold icy water.

The manager reached under his desk and pulled out a small white towel. "Here, dry your face up with this," he said, handing the towel to me. I took it carefully and dried my face and hair, but I kept my viewpoint focused on him to make doubly sure that he was real and would not disappear.

"As I was saying," the manager continued, "the doll has been testing you ever since you bought her. You are still undergoing her test, which is to find out where exactly she is hiding at this very moment."

The manager paused to pull out a cigar and a match from his suit pocket. He lit the match, lit the cigar, put out the match with his fingers, put the cigar in his mouth, and puffed once. He went on, "When you find her again, ask her for her name. Then I will notify you of your next job either personally, or through an associate."

I decided to play along with the manager's little game without asking too many questions. After all, this 'job' was actually quite interesting. It seemed like I was a playable character in one of Mark's video games, where the object of the game was to search for an annoying target (in this case, the doll) hiding in multiple places.

"Alright," I said to the manager, setting the small towel on the desk, "I will try to find the doll."

The manager threw the still-lit cigar behind him, and said to me, "I'm happy that you decided to cooperate with us without hesitation, Omar." He pulled out a key from under his desk and threw it to me. I caught the key in both of my hands. "This is the key to your office. It's on the second floor. Your door is marked with a number 3. You won't miss it." He got up and extended his right hand to me, saying, "Thanks again for agreeing to be a part of our team, Omar." I got up, smiled blankly, and firmly shook his hand. As I turned around to exit the manager's office, he called out, "And by the way, people here call me Face. I suggest you call me by that name, too." I turned to him, nodded my head, and then turned around again to head out the door.

I walked past the brilliant hallway containing the hordes of greenery, and walked into the open elevator. After the doors closed, I pressed the button numbered '2' to activate the lift to go down to the second floor.

The Office

When the elevator reached the second floor, I exited and looked around. The second floor hallway looked like the standard hotel hallways I had seen in foreign countries, during my family's vacation travels when we stayed in average hotels. The floor was made of a red carpet that was stained, probably due to drinks such as orange juice or coffee spilled on the floor many times mistakenly. The walls were beige color, and six brown doors were lined up one after another along the hallway. *What a waste of space,* I thought. There were only six office rooms in this hallway when, judging by the hallway's immense length, there could have been at least *twenty* offices!

I walked up to the door marked with a golden number 3. I inserted the old-fashioned key into the key hole, twisted it until I heard a click, then opened the door, and walked in. The room was dark, so I felt for a light switch on the side of the wall to turn the lights on.

With the lights on now, I saw that this room did not look like an office at all. A king-sized bed with a dark-blue blanket and pillow sat against the right wall, with a little chocolate-colored bedside table sitting next to it. On the left side of the room was an open door which led to a small kitchen with a black-and-white microwave oven resting on a wooden cabinet at the entrance of the open doorway. Next to the opened kitchen door was a comfortable-looking dark-green chair with a tall lamp next to it. A desk with two chairs sat at the end of the room straight ahead from me. A telephone sat on this desk. The carpeted floor was a dark-blue color.

This looked more like a *hotel* room than an office!

I swallowed hard, but did not hesitate. I kept myself calm and bore in mind that the manager nicknamed 'Face' – *my* manager – seemed to have a lot of faith in me working for his company. So it should not surprise me that he gave me a very comfortable office to do my work. Perhaps he put a bed in my office in the event that I would have to stay working for more than a day. I was aware that some jobs are like that; there would be times when you had to work long therefore it was better to have a place to stay and sleep closer to work, instead of going back home late then not getting enough sleep for the next day.

Suddenly, I heard a telephone ringing. It was an office phone that was sitting on the desk with the two chairs. I picked up the phone after three rings. A familiar voice questioned, "Hello? Is that Omar?" It was the voice of Face.

"Yes, it's me," I replied.

"Oh good, you made it to your office. This is your manager, Face, in case you didn't recognize by now. I tried to make your working environment as comfortable for you as possible, hope you like it. And don't worry about your door closing and locking on its own. All the doors on the second floor are programmed to automatically close ten seconds after being left open."

I thought about it, and then silently accepted the scenario as normal. An enigmatic company such as this one would logically have strict security measures and a deceiving outer surface, in order to operate properly and without security breaches. Besides, I doubt many people would even be interested in robbing the place based on the plain appearance of the company from the outside.

Face continued, "Why don't you lie down on your bed for a while? In fact, I'll give you the rest of the day off. I'll have you start your job tomorrow."

"Alright, thank you…Face," I nervously replied, feeling awkward addressing my manager directly without a title such as 'Mister Face,' as that sounded like a ludicrous title.

Face laughed a little, then said, "Don't be afraid to call me Face, everyone working here calls me Face!" He fell silent for a moment, and then his tone changed a bit. "One more thing, Omar, you won't be going home tonight. You will be staying here for as long as it takes, so that you can be fully successful while working in our company. And don't worry about your parents; I will call them tomorrow and tell them that you will be staying with us to work for the company." Then his tone changed back to the comedic tone I heard from him after his little laugh. "So don't worry about a thing, Omar! You'll do fine with us. Bye, talk to you tomorrow!"

After he hung up, I softly placed the phone back on its receiver. Normally, people in my situation would have panicked and started running to the door, frantically banging on it with their fists and screaming for help to arrive, just like those unfortunate characters in movies and television shows that get freaked out when they get trapped in a room. But I stayed calm because I did not feel trapped in here; I actually felt *welcomed* somehow, considering the negativity I had experienced recently from my father and from Mark.

Feeling relieved, I plopped myself on my back onto the huge soft bed. It was the most comfortable bed I had ever lied on; I felt like I was lying on dozens of tiny soft pillows, when in reality I was lying on a mattress covered with a sheet and a blanket. I slowly closed my eyes, and eventually fell into a deep sleep.

Awake

I woke up realizing that I slept on my back. I felt a weight that was on top of my stomach, something very light in weight. Without getting up from the bed, I lowered my chin as close to my chest as possible, and I narrowed my eyes to have a look.

The red-haired *doll* was literally seated on my stomach, its plush cotton legs facing straight forward. The blank cyan blue eyes on its seemingly forever-smiling face stared at me.

I quickly jumped out of bed. My sudden movement sent the doll flying into the wall next to the bed, and then it plopped soundlessly onto the floor. I stood over the doll, just staring into its face for a few moments, thinking.

Then I remembered something: Face had told me to ask the doll for its name (or as he put it: Her name) whenever I managed to see it again. So I asked it, in an awkward manner, "What is your…name?"

Suddenly, the small doll leapt onto its two soft plush feet, standing straight, and I heard a squeaky but clearly audible voice answer, "Chibi!"

After hearing her response, I laughed. The name of this doll was very fitting, since the word 'chibi' is actually the pronunciation of a Japanese word meaning 'small,' and she was only the size of my hand. I acquired this knowledge from when I watched Japanese animated shows in my younger days. I continued laughing; the situation was all too bizarre to stifle my laughter!

Chibi's facial expression actually started to change; her mouth turned from a smile to a frown. "Why are you laughing?" she asked me in that squeaky little-girl voice.

I stopped laughing, and replied to her, "It's your name, it suits you perfectly. It's too obvious!"

Chibi put her tiny plush hands to her hips, and said, "Well, it's not my fault that my name is Chibi and I happen to be small! You're mean!" She walked up to my left foot, and kicked it with her plushy right foot. I did not feel anything from her kick at all. I smiled and picked her up from the floor to the level of my face.

"I'm sorry, Chibi, I was only joking," I apologized. She loosened from my soft grip and jumped back down to the floor, landing on her feet.

"Okay, now you passed the first test. Congratulations!" Chibi commented. She clapped her plush hands, making only soft patting sounds that I barely heard. I smiled and sat down on the bed. "Face might soon tell you about your next job, or someone else will come in here to let you know," she continued. "But for now, how about I make you some breakfast? I know how to cook!"

As soon as I heard the word 'breakfast,' I pulled out my mobile phone from my pocket to check the time. It was eight o'clock in the morning, which meant that I had fallen asleep very early yesterday. I was not at all surprised, since I was normally a heavy sleeper and since the bed in my 'office' was comfortable enough to drown me to sleep.

If another person was in my place right now, he/she would have probably been scared to death by this talking doll, just like those characters in the movies that are never ready to witness anything supernatural. Most people nowadays would not wish to explore anything outside their realm of everyday ordinary life. I am not like those kinds of people; I love seeing different things happen around me, instead of seeing the same generic stuff happening every single day. I truly enjoyed my engagements with the unusual.

"What kind of breakfast are you going to make?" I asked Chibi.

She replied, "Anything you want! Pancakes, waffles, eggs…I can make the eggs scrambled or sunny-side up…"

"Pancakes?" I quickly suggested. "Two pancakes, but I'll pour the syrup on them."

Chibi then said, "Hey, *I* am cooking! *I* will pour the syrup! You can watch me make them. Follow me!" She scuttled into the kitchen, and I followed her.

The kitchen did not look really special; in addition to the microwave oven on the cabinet I saw earlier, there were also the usual things I have seen before in standard kitchens: a refrigerator, a stove, a sink, and another cabinet (there was a door next to this other cabinet, with a label on the door that said 'bathroom'). Chibi jumped from the floor all the way onto the cabinet that was next to the stove. I noticed the following things about Chibi: She can walk, talk, change her facial expression, and jump to high places effortlessly. They are obviously things that normal dolls cannot do, since normal dolls are lifeless. Chibi was full of life indeed.

She turned her face toward me. "Um…actually, I may need you to help me a little bit," she squeaked shyly. "I'm very small, so it would take long for me to reach for everything in here. You get the milk and four eggs from the fridge, and I'll get the flour and frying pan and other stuff." I followed her instructions and opened the fridge. Aside from milk and eggs, I saw an assortment of other foods and drinks: several bottles of water, condiments, maple syrup, and small clear plastic containers, each of which contained vegetables and fruits, as well as what appeared to be bologna and different types of cheeses. Face was already treating me in good hospitality.

I took out the milk and four eggs and set them on the cabinet. I saw that Chibi had already gotten out the flour and frying pan, as well as a plastic spatula, and a big wooden spoon and mixing bowl for blending together the necessary ingredients. Chibi was somehow holding the huge wooden spoon in both hands with ease. I smiled; she looked like a living character from a kids cartoon show!

"Now crack the eggs into the bowl, add the milk and flour, and I'll stir everything," she told me instructively. I did what she told me to do, and suddenly, she hopped up high to the ceiling and, while pointing the wooden spoon downwards, dived towards the center of the bowl but then stopped and hovered in the air a few inches above the bowl. *Magical*, I thought to myself, observing this uncanny sight. I quickly stepped back to avoid the contents of the bowl splashing onto my clothes.

Still floating above the mixing bowl with the spoon still in her grip, she spun in a perfect 360-degree angle to mix everything in the bowl. After a few more spins, she stopped. "Okay, all done. Now I'll pour the stuff into the frying pan," she said to me. Then ordered, "Turn the stove on full heat, and put the pan on the stove." I did what I was told, and saw her easily lift the big mixing bowl above her head with both her hands. Two more noticeable things about Chibi observed so far: she can also fly and float around, and she had enough strength to lift something heavier than her.

She poured some of the mixed ingredients into the pan, set the bowl down, and picked up the spatula to start shaping the first pancake. After shaping and flipping it, she used the spatula to pick up the pancake and place it on a free plate which sat next to the stove. She then picked up the bowl again, poured the rest of the ingredients into the pan, and repeated the process to make my second pancake. After she was done, she set the second pancake onto my first one that lay on the plate.

"Now Omar, you can get the syrup out of the fridge and pour as much of it as you want on your pancakes!" she said cheerfully. I got the maple syrup and poured some on my pancakes, and went back to my bed/office room with the plate of my breakfast. As I placed my plate on the desk, Chibi called out from the kitchen, "Hey Omar, you forgot something!" I looked and saw her walking up to me with a silver fork in her hands. "Thanks, Chibi," I said to her before taking the fork from her.

Then I asked her, "Why didn't you just fly over to me to give me the fork?"

Chibi replied, "Well, if I fly around too much I start feeling really tired and weak, so I can't do it all the time. But anyway, I think walking on my own two legs is great, I can get my leg muscles stronger!" She then began to jump up and down, her red flower skirt twirling with each jump. I smiled and nodded to her response, and then I started eating my breakfast.

*****

"So how were the pancakes?" Chibi asked after I finished eating. She was sitting on the bed, having waited for me to be finished with my breakfast.

I responded, "Very good," then said in a sarcastic manner, "I never knew that dolls had knowledge about cooking pancakes."

There was a little silence, and then I saw Chibi quickly jump to the ceiling and land on my empty plate. She looked at me, frowning and with her hands on her hips, and said, "Hey! Are you making fun of me?" I was going to reply to her, but then she looked down at her feet, lifted her right foot up, and examined the bottom of her foot. It was covered with some of the gooey brown maple syrup that was left on my plate. "Now my feet are all dirty!" she cried in an annoyed tone. "I need to be washed now."

She jumped off the desk and landed on the floor. I got up from my chair and looked at her. "Why don't you just wash yourself in the kitchen sink or in the bathroom?" I asked.

Chibi replied, "Omar, this is *your* room. I will go wash myself in *my own* room! Besides, my job here is done for now." She walked to my office door and stopped. Since the door handle was too high up for her, she floated up toward the handle to open the door, and drifted outside of the room. She stopped and turned around, and said to me with a smiling expression from her unmoving mouth. "Bye, Omar! See you soon!" She waved at me with her plush right hand for ten seconds. Awkwardly, I smiled and waved back at her.

Then the door closed, and I heard the familiar clicking sound which meant the door automatically locked.

I walked back to my bed and let myself fall backwards onto it. So Chibi also has a room in this building. That made sense, since she is one of the employees of this company. I wondered what other weird coworkers I would meet next.

As I thought about this, I had fallen asleep once again. What can I say? I fall asleep easily, which could be one of my best or worst attributes. In this case, it was definitely one of my worst, since I was supposed to be awake for a notification from either my manager Face or someone else. Luckily, I only slept for about twenty minutes. Upon hearing the office telephone ringing, I woke up. I looked at my cell for the time. *Thank goodness it's still the same day*, I thought, after looking at the date on my cell phone. Feeling annoyed at the ringing tone of the office telephone, I got up and answered it, only to hear the person on the other end hang up on me. Then all of a sudden, I heard the door open. I saw a tall figure walk into my office.

Interlude

It is time to take a little break from my story. It is time to briefly return to my current state. Once I had turned on the lights in the shack, I saw a thick book with blank pages and a cylindrical container holding pens of many colors, all sitting on a little wooden table. Face had told me that my assignment was to write down my story once I had arrived at the shack, and he, or possibly one of his associates, was generous enough to leave this book and these pens here for my convenience. If it was one of Face's associates who had left these here for me, perhaps it was Chibi who had done it. Or maybe it was that person who had entered my room after I had met Chibi for the first time…

In any case, whoever had done this was very kind. All of the company's employees were kind to each other (so much so that even the manager Face refers to all of them as his 'associates' rather than his employees), and to me. But they were not so friendly towards people whose personalities consisted of ignorance and callousness. These types of people would never be hired into the company to begin with, according to Face. That was perhaps the only problem with the company, which would explain why the number of main employees working in it are far and few between. But somehow the company still manages to make a whole lot of money to keep itself – and its staff – in existence.

Now is the time for me to stop rambling. I shall continue with my story, I shall keep on writing at an intensive pace in order to not waste any more time. I hope that you, my dear reader, will bear with me as my story continues to unfold.

Doctor

I took a good look at the person who walked into my office. He was a tall but well-built man, wearing a white laboratory coat over a black vest and black trousers. His face had some sort of face-paint on it: black paint all over his face except for a big number six painted in the middle of his forehead in a red color. And his eyes were bright white; they had no pupil or iris, just the white sclera. And his hair was worn in short dreadlocks. He was holding a black suitcase in his left hand.

I could tell he was affiliated with the company because of the identification card clipped on his lab coat; a passport-sized head shot photograph of him was on the left side of the card, and the company name was at the top of the card written in capital letters. And his name and other details filled the rest of the card.

"Omar," the tall man began, "my name is Doctor Six, pleased to meet you." He extended his right hand to me. This man that introduced himself as 'Doctor Six' was wearing black open-finger gloves.

I shook his hand and replied, "Nice to meet you, too."

He smiled and then said to me, "Congratulations, you have passed the first test. Pardon Face for not fully explaining your occupation at our company; he tends to be quite cryptic when he instructs new employees about their tasks, in order to test them for their inner skill sets. Allow me to thoroughly explain to you your duties to the company."

He pulled out one of the chairs that were next to my desk, sat down and placed the suitcase upright next to him on the floor, and motioned to me to sit down on the other chair. I sat down and listened to him attentively.

"Before I explain what you have to do in this company, keep in mind that this is not an ordinary company. Our business does not have a fixed main branch anywhere in the world. In a literal and physical sense, we are constantly moving around the world. We are in this city right now, and our next location is unknown at this stage.

"Because of the continuous mobility of the company as a whole, as well as the desire of the company mission to be kept a secret from the rest of the world, the name of the company must always change. As you must have noticed from the billboard outside, right above the entrance of this building, the current name of our company is Ruof Researchers Corporation."

I childishly raised my hand in an attempt to ask Doctor Six a question. He said, "Yes Omar, you have a question?"

I replied, "Yes. Does this company have a website on the internet?"

Doctor Six answered, "Yes, however, you will not be able to find it as a public access on the World Wide Web. The company has its own internet server which I will tell you about another day. But for now, let me tell you about your job role in our company:

"Your role in this company is to assist fellow employees in their missions, and write a report on those missions. These reports will be useful for keeping the records of the company's actions, as well as helping its staff learn from prior mistakes in these missions. Basically, your job is based on teamwork and the ability to accurately observe details in the missions. Our company's goal is to make the world a better place to live in, by allowing the good to flourish and eliminating what we classify as 'evil'."

He picked up the suitcase from the floor and handed it to me. "Your writing equipment is all in this suitcase: a custom-made laptop computer specially engineered by yours truly, a stack of blank A4 paper, a notebook, and pens," he told me. I took the suitcase from him. Then he added, "You can start working on your first report after assisting me in my mission. Leave the suitcase here, and come with me."

I left my suitcase on my desk and followed him outside my office room. Doctor Six pressed the 'down' button next to the elevator door, and eventually the door opened. We both stepped inside, the door closing after our entry, and waited until the elevator reached the bottom.

When we reached the ground floor, the elevator door opened and we both walked out, him leading me outside. I noticed that the female receptionist from yesterday was absent from her desk. *Perhaps she went to the restroom and would quickly come back,* I thought.

Doctor Six stopped next to the driver's side door of the beat-up, gray-colored van that was parked in the handicap parking space. I smiled as I realized that this van was a part of this mysterious company, and that the driver who deliberately parked on this restricted space was Doctor Six himself. He took off a police ticket that was stuck to the driver's side window, and looked at it. He grimaced and ripped the ticket with both gloved hands, saying, "The police should learn that a mere ticket will not guarantee that the driver will follow their rules in the future." He cupped his hands carrying the ticket confetti, brought his hands close to his mouth, and blew the ripped ticket pieces away into the gray cemented environment of the empty parking lot.

He then reached inside his coat pocket, fumbling for the key to the van. He pulled out the key, and attached to it was a keychain ornament that looked familiar. It was Chibi!

"Ow! Doctor, you're hurting me! You're pulling my hair!" Chibi screamed in her shrill little girl voice. One side of the small chain that connected Chibi to the car key was somehow wrapped around her hair in a ponytail fashion. I laughed, and Doctor Six turned to me while slowly cradling Chibi and the key in his right hand.

He smiled and said, "Oh yes, I forgot to mention that Chibi will be accompanying us in this mission. Isn't that right, Chibi?" I saw Chibi looking at him with a frown, and sensed that she was angry with me because I laughed at her embarrassing situation.

But then, her frown changed to a smile, and she replied to him, "Yes, Doctor. I'll do my best."

Doctor Six unlocked the driver's side door manually with the old-fashioned car key and stepped into the van. "Hop in, Omar," he ordered. I walked around to the other side of the van to the passenger's side, and while doing so I noticed that my car was nowhere to be seen in the lot.

When I got into the van, I asked the doctor, "I parked my car in this parking lot, but I don't see it anymore—"

"Don't worry about your car, it is safe and sound," he assured me. "Yesterday, your car was towed by one of our company's employees and placed in a highly secure warehouse. We will go to that warehouse later today."

He buckled up his safety belt, put the key in the ignition, turned the key, and the engine roared loudly. "Weeee!" Chibi exclaimed cheerfully while dangling from the car key. Doctor Six patted her head, and then concentrated at reversing the van and pulling out of the parking lot to begin our mission.

The Drive

While Doctor Six drove us to the location where our mission was to take place (with the radio off; I guessed the doctor did not like listening to music), I was thinking deeply about a few things. Firstly, why were the doctor's eyes fully white without any visible pupils or irises? Secondly, what medical field was the doctor specialized in exactly? And thirdly, what would he and Chibi be doing in this mission that I would have to assist with?

I forced myself to ask these questions to the doctor, beginning with the first, "So, doctor, what happened to your eyes?"

Doctor Six glanced at me for two seconds, and then fixed his pupil-less eyes to the road in front of us. He answered, "That is a very good question, Omar. My eyes were previously normal-looking, but due to a terrible car accident some years back, my eyes had to be surgically enhanced, in such a way that the colored parts of my eyes had to be made white, just like the white area of my eyes."

I purposely kept silent for three seconds, and then I said to him without looking at him, "I'm sorry for hearing about this." I heard Chibi sob lightly; she also seemed to feel a little bit of sadness after hearing about the doctor's unfortunate condition.

Doctor Six replied, "No worries, Omar. Believe it or not, ever since my eyes were made this way, I saw things even better than before my accident. I am actually glad that my eyes are the way they are now; I always feel a sense of uniqueness whenever I look at my face in the mirror. And besides, Face hired me after my accident and liked it that I showed a positive attitude about my new look. I have to keep my face painted, though, for the sake of confidentiality in the company missions."

Now that the first question was out of the way, I asked him my second question, "And what do you specialize in, doctor?"

He replied, "Medicine. I am in charge of the manufacture of medicines that help cure various pains and diseases of fellow employees. However, I only provide these medicines if employees are *really* in need of them. I strictly discourage prescribing medications to staff members on a constant basis, as the medicines tend to become addicting if an overdose occurs. However just in case, I created antidotes for all my medicines to counter the negative effects caused by overdose."

Doctor Six's explanation of his occupation was very interesting to me; I strongly felt that he played a large role in the company. If I knew him better, I would have looked up to him as if he was my mentor. But since I only recently joined the company, I felt it was better not to rush into things.

Finally, I coerced myself to ask my third question to Doctor Six, "One last question, Doctor. What are you and Chibi going to be doing in this mission?"

Doctor Six laughed out loud, and told me, "Don't worry about us; we have our own orders to carry out. You, on the other hand, should just do as I say once we reach our destination." Then the doctor's tone of voice bleakly changed as he added, "Don't lag behind like the previous staff member did before you. He sadly passed away during one of his missions with me. I told him to run faster to catch up to me, but he was too far behind and then he was run over…" The doctor's voice trailed off. I saw him place his right hand on his forehead while his left hand supported the steering wheel. I heard Chibi utter sadly in her tiny voice.

"I wish I was there to help him, Doctor. I wish I came along with you that time!"

Doctor Six paused for a few seconds, and continued, "Omar, that other employee formerly resided in your office many years ago in the room numbered 3. Face had nicknamed him 'The Third One,' or 'Third' for short. Ever since The Third One died, office number 3 was never again used. Face had decided that only a person with as much good spirit in his heart as The Third One would be allowed to stay in office number 3, and he saw enough potential in you to let you use that office. Moreover, he even decided to withhold the nickname 'The Third One' until he can give it to another promising and eligible candidate.

"In fact, Face had given all employees of the company, including himself, nicknames that replaced their real names. As a rule, each and every employee must have their original names replaced by a nickname. Once an employee is given a nickname, he or she must be addressed by that name and must also accept that name as his or her main name. My current name is obviously a nickname, and Chibi's name is also a nickname. We all had real names before we were employed by the company."

I thought for a moment about what the doctor said, and then I asked him, "So how come I didn't get a nickname yet?"

Doctor Six replied, "Because Face has not yet decided what your nickname should be. However, after proving yourself by completing this mission, he will surely choose a nickname for you. And based on the fact that Face let you stay in office number 3, I am sure your nickname will indeed be 'The Third One.'"

"Okay, thanks for telling me all of this, Doctor. I am really learning a lot so far," I said to him.

"Not a problem, Omar," he replied, and then he looked outside the windshield of the van. "I think we're almost to our destination, about three minutes or so."

After he had said that, things quieted down in the van. In silence, I felt excited. I couldn't wait to find out what my upcoming nickname would be.

Arrival

"Okay, this is our stop," Doctor Six announced. He pulled in front of what appeared to be an old mansion, located in a neighborhood I was unfamiliar with. The mansion was colored a light green, with black tinted windows on its second story. The view of the bottom half of the mansion was blocked by a tall and wide brown wall, which surrounded the mansion on all sides. Even the decoration-less black gate of the house did not offer a view of the bottom floor of the mansion; it was a fully walled sliding gate, not the common transparent fence-style gates which allow people to at least have a minimal glimpse of the entrance. In addition to the second storey of the mansion, four tall palm trees were also seen surpassing the height of the great wall.

Doctor Six switched off the engine of the van, took the key and Chibi in his hand, and got out of the van. I also stepped outside, and took a good look around. *This neighborhood is strange*, I thought. Although I knew most of the residential neighborhoods in my city, I had never noticed this one before. I saw other houses around me, but they seemed abandoned and no sound was heard from them. This place was too quiet; even during this time in the morning (the time was 9:30 am), neighborhoods like this would have people walking around or cars driving by, hustling and bustling to school or to work. It felt like nobody lived here.

Doctor Six walked up to me, with Chibi trailing behind him with the key still attached to her hair like a ponytail. As Chibi followed him, the key dragged on the ground making an annoying metallic scratching sound. Doctor Six turned his head toward Chibi and told her sternly, "Chibi, please hide the key in your hair so that it doesn't make those unsettling noises. We do not want to attract unwanted attention."

I chuckled after the doctor had said that to her. Chibi looked up at me with an angry expression, but then looked away from me and stuck the front part of the key in her hair. The key now looked like a ridiculously big metallic ornament in her hair.

Doctor Six looked to me again and said, "All right, Omar, we have to get inside this mansion. You and Chibi stay back, I will ring the doorbell."

The doctor walked towards the right side of the big gate. He pressed the doorbell button with one finger, and the bell chimed. A few seconds later, the gate slid open a little bit, and a very short casually dressed bald man walked out of the small opening. Chibi quickly hid behind me before the man showed himself.

"Yes? What you want?" the short man started in a broken English accent. I guessed he was the doorman or watchman of the mansion.

Doctor Six responded to the man, "Hello, my name is Doctor Six. I came here to see Mister Jassim because he is sick today. Has he informed you about me coming here?"

The short man shook his head and was going to say something, but suddenly, Doctor Six pulled a red cloth out from his lab coat pocket. The man was too slow for the doctor's fast reflexes; Doctor Six quickly dashed to the man and gently smothered his face with the cloth. When the doctor pulled the cloth away, the man fell to the ground, eyes closed, and breathing softly as if he was sleeping.

I was honestly shocked at what I saw. The doctor actually lied to someone and made that someone unconscious against his will. Actions that I did not expect to see from him at all!

As Doctor Six put the cloth back into his pocket, I said to him, "Doctor, what did you just do? I thought you said the company did things for the good of the world! Just now you lied to this innocent man, and made him unconscious—"

"This man is not completely innocent," Doctor Six firmly interjected, "he works for a gang that terrorizes people from this neighborhood and many others. This mansion is the gang's hideout." He pulled the sleeping man aside and away from the gate, and turned to me and said, "And don't worry, I did not hurt this man; I merely put him to sleep using a tranquilizing chemical compound embedded within the cloth. He should wake up whenever he hears a loud sound. Now follow me, you two."

We followed him into the mansion's outdoor entrance. He motioned to me to close the gate, and I closed it behind me. I looked around and was amazed at what I saw.

The front entrance of the mansion was a spacious driveway, with graffiti everywhere, including on the ground! Vulgar language was written in various languages on the mansion's first storey surface wall and main door, and its lower windows had blood-red graffiti sprayed on them. The lower parts of the palm trees were spray-painted with random colors, destroying the natural brown colors of the palm trees' stems. Even the two vehicles parked in the driveway, a large black sport utility vehicle and a red sports car had some graffiti sprayed on their bodies.

Chibi jumped on the sports car and stood there for a moment, then exclaimed, "This place is so ugly! How can anyone want to live here?"

Doctor Six responded to her, "Only gangs with no morals and no sense of order would want to live here, and they should be sitting inside the mansion."

Chibi jumped off of the car and back on the ground, asking, "What if they try to attack us when we get inside?"

Doctor Six replied, "I will deal with them if they try to attack me or any one of you. Leave the defensive maneuvers to me."

The doctor led the way to the spray-painted door of the mansion, and Chibi and I followed him. He slowly twisted the doorknob, and pushed the door open. It was not locked. I assumed the doorman we had met earlier had carelessly left it unlocked.

Doctor Six stepped inside, with me and Chibi closely behind him. The entrance what could have been the living room contained no furniture except for a long sofa which was stained with graffiti, and a giant chandelier which hung in the center of the room's ceiling (which provided the lights for visibility; the light was on when we entered the room). Empty aluminum soft drink cans, plastic bottles, and cigarette butts were scattered throughout this room, and graffiti was marked everywhere on the carpeted floor. *This gang probably named themselves the Graffiti Gang,* I thought.

Chibi startled me when she suddenly jumped and landed in a sitting position on my right shoulder. "Ewww, this place is so dirty! I don't want to get my feet dirty," Chibi exclaimed shrilly after she landed on my shoulder.

Doctor Six then turned back to us, put his index finger to his mouth, and whispered, "Ssshhh, we have to be very quiet so that they don't suddenly attack us. They should be in a room upstairs."

There was a big stairway on our right. We walked in that direction, with the doctor still leading the way. The stairs were wooden but surprisingly sturdy, making minimal sounds as we trudged towards the second floor of the mansion.

Finally, once we reached the top, we heard sounds in one of the rooms. The sounds were coming from the last room to our left. "Alright, Omar, the mission will begin as soon as we enter that room at the end of the hallway. You stay behind me at all times and observe what goes on, and I will do the rest," Doctor Six ordered, "and Chibi, you make yourself hidden so that the gang members do not see you." Chibi obeyed his order by climbing down from my shoulder and into my right pocket. My right thigh felt slightly ticklish after Chibi wriggled her way into my pocket, but I didn't let that distract me from the mission that I was about to take part in.

We walked up to the door, and Doctor Six pressed his ear against it to listen, as we all heard the gruff sounds of a group of men chatting. Then slowly and with great caution, he knocked on the door four times.

Confrontation

A few seconds after Doctor Six knocked on the door, it was opened by a bulky tanned man wearing black army-styled boots, brown khakis and an extra-large sized white shirt with an offensive phrase printed on it. He had a wide scarred face that showed an expression of hostility the moment he laid his eyes upon the doctor and me (thank goodness Chibi stayed hiding in my pocket). "Who are you?" he asked in a deep harsh voice.

The doctor replied to him, "I am Doctor Six. I came here to discuss the neighborhood takeover plan with Mister Jassim." He pointed at me, continuing, "I brought an expert associate with me just in case any problems arise."

The huge gangster smiled when he saw me, probably thinking to himself that I was no match for him in a fight, and then said, "I was not informed of anybody meeting Jassim here today, but you can come in." He stepped away from the doorway, and gestured for us to enter. We walked in.

The big room that we walked into looked and smelled filthy. Two torn-up leather sofas lay against the left wall of the room, and on the right was a long rectangular wooden table onto which lay crumpled papers, stacks of empty soft drink cans, and many cigarette butts. The floor was covered with various items that would have been found in a dumpster: empty bottles of the glass and plastic variety, candy wrappers, plastic bags, and wasted chunks of food. The room stank of rotten meat and moldy bread.

There were three more people in the room, all inhabiting one of the sofas. One was a scrawny teenage boy wearing a blue cap, white sneakers, blue sports shorts, and an oversized orange shirt with the phrase 'Number One' printed on it. The second person was a shirtless muscle-bound man wearing torn jeans and was barefoot. The third person was a man wearing a bright white suit with a pink tie, black dress shoes, and a pink trilby on his head. All three of them were sitting next to each other, side by side.

The man in the white suit stood up and said rudely, "Who are you and why are you here?" After he had said that, his comrades quickly got up and stood next to his sides, the teenaged gangster on his left, and the muscled gangster on his right. I heard the door behind us slam shut, and I looked back to see that the tanned gangster stood in front of the door, cracking the knuckles of his right hand using his left, grinning at me.

I turned to look at Doctor Six. He seemed calm and unbothered by the hostility surrounding us. After a few seconds, he finally spoke up, "Jassim, I am here to put an end to your gang's merciless actions against the innocent people of this neighborhood. If you don't cooperate with me right now, things could get ugly."

Jassim, the man dressed in the bright white suit, responded in a broken English accent with a violent tone in his voice, "What we do in this neighborhood is none of your business! You are not from this neighborhood, so you can't do anything against us!"

Suddenly, I felt my arms being grabbed and pulled behind my back. I heard the tanned gangster say, "Don't move." I stayed still in order to avoid getting hurt by this man; his grip on my arms felt strong enough to break a steel chain in one go.

Doctor Six put his hand in his pocket and quickly pulled out a small vial filled with a gray-colored substance, and smashed it on the ground in front of Jassim. A smoky cloud engulfed the entire room in a matter of seconds. I heard the gangsters coughing rapidly, and felt the tanned gangster's grip on my arms disappear. I looked back and saw that he had plopped face down on the floor. I put my hand over my nose and mouth and looked for the doctor, but I could not see him anywhere due to the smoke. "Doctor, where are you?" I yelled, my voice slightly muffled by my hand covering my mouth. Then I realized I should not have said a word, as that garnered the gang's attention towards me. I saw a figure running to me amidst the smoke, a figure too small and skinny to be the doctor. It was the teenage gangster. He had a wooden stick in his hand and raised it in an attempt to hit me on the head. When he was just inches away from me, Doctor Six appeared out of nowhere and body-speared the boy to the ground in an American football-styled tackle. I felt Chibi get out of my pocket, and saw her run to the doctor.

The doctor picked her up and told her, "Quickly, Chibi, open the door to this room to let the smoke out. This smoke will become toxic for us if left enclosed in this room twenty seconds more."

"Okay, Doc!" Chibi replied obediently and actively jumped off of the doctor's hand. I noticed she didn't cough or cover her mouth. She didn't seem to be affected at all by the smoke around us. I guessed this was because she was a doll and not a human being.

Chibi ran to the door and opened it wide enough for the smoke to flow out of the room. I looked around and saw that the tanned gangster and teenage gangster were out cold, and the muscled gangster and Jassim were on their knees, conscious and still coughing. Doctor Six got up and shouted to me and Chibi, "Run, you two! I'll be right behind you!" We followed his orders and ran outside the room, with Chibi outrunning me. She was amazingly fast, I thought. She already disappeared from my line of vision.

I looked back and saw Doctor Six catch up to me. We both ran alongside each other down the stairs, through the ground floor of the mansion, and out onto the graffiti driveway. I saw the gate already opened; Chibi had opened it for us. I saw Chibi standing outside the half-opened gate, next to the still-sleeping doorman, waving at us. When we arrived to her, she announced, "Doctor, we have a problem! The van's not here anymore!" And indeed, both of us looked at the spot where the van was parked, and it was gone. Doctor Six said, "Don't worry, Chibi. Face told me beforehand that he would send another member of the staff with a spare key to drive the van somewhere else, so that it doesn't get towed away by police. We don't want any evidence of our whereabouts to be found out by the authorities or anybody connected with this gang."

I heard loud profanity being shouted behind us, and when I looked back, I saw the muscled gangster running towards us with a metal pipe. I was going to run, but Doctor Six gripped my shoulder with his hand. "Wait, Omar, there's our getaway car." He pointed to my right, and I saw a classy black sedan without a license plate driving towards us. I saw a hand waving at us from the driver's side. The car stopped sharply next to us, and I saw a familiar face: The driver who came to our rescue was the gas station cashier from the old station I was at two days ago. She was wearing a dark-blue beret. I felt a sense of relief when I saw her.

"Get in, people!" the cashier ordered. The doctor opened the rear door and climbed in first, then Chibi, then me. I closed the door and locked it just as the muscled gangster reached the car. He attempted to pull the door open, but it was no use since it was now locked. The cashier pushed the accelerator hard which strongly pushed the car forward. The sudden jerk of the powerful luxury sedan being pushed forward also made the muscled gangster lose his grip on the car's door handle, and made him fall and tumble to the ground on his stomach. We sped away from the mansion.

"We got away from those weirdoes! Yay!" Chibi cheered. She jumped happily, between Doctor Six and me, on the spacious back seat of the luxury sedan. The doctor then grabbed her gently and covered her mouth to keep her quiet. Then he asked the cashier, "So did you notify the police so they could have a look at the mansion?" The cashier replied, "Yes I did, the police should arrive on the scene in a minute or two." The doctor then said, "Good, once the police find out about the mansion and its occupants, they will arrest the gang members for their crimes against the neighborhood."

Doctor Six then turned to me and said, "Until now, that gang we met back there had posed as a harmless fun-loving gang of the neighborhood whenever they were faced by the police. Naturally, the police allowed the gang to exist in the neighborhood as they did not find any evidence to penalize the gang for crimes. To make matters worse, the residents of that neighborhood were too terrified to complain and as a result kept silent, so the police assumed that the gang was friendly to the neighborhood. But once the police arrive and witness the condition of the mansion and evidence of their criminal activities, they will arrest that gang and have their hideout torn down."

I nodded to him, but then I said to him, "You hurt the teenager back there really badly when you tackled him. What if you broke his ribs or something—"

"He was not an innocent person," Doctor Six interrupted. "Even before he had joined Jassim's gang, he had committed many bad crimes, things that you would not want to know about. He deserves to be heavily punished, and I don't consider my tackling him as punishment enough. It's better that he be in the hands of the police, so that he can learn from his mistakes while in jail."

I fell silent for some time, and then the doctor put his hand on my shoulder and said, "Sometimes, Omar, you have to overlook certain things for the good of the situation. That gang member being a teenager is not enough reason for me to forgive him for his mistakes, because he was too far into his mistakes and could not be corrected by non-authoritative means. If just one troublemaker's crimes are ignored, then the crimes of other criminals will eventually be ignored due to the needless sympathy of the narrow-minded masses. In our company, we must abide by the rules in order to be successfully righteous in the end of our missions."

After the doctor's speech, I nodded once more and kept silent. I had many questions in my mind, but I decided to keep them to myself and wait patiently until the petrol station cashier took us to our next destination.

Destination

The petrol station cashier stopped in front of the gate of a large warehouse located in a busy industrial complex. I recognized this place; I came to this area a few months ago to change the tires of my car because they were getting worn out. The cashier honked the horn twice, and the warehouse gate opened. She drove inside, the gate closing behind us after entry.

The warehouse was brightly lit up by the high fluorescent ceiling lights, illuminating the place in an off-white vanilla-colored brightness. Several cars were parked straight at the end of the warehouse: including my very own car, there was a white limousine, a big beige-colored pickup truck with camouflage markings, a tow truck, an ambulance without emergency markings on it, and four black luxury sedans which were the same model as the car we were currently sitting in. Other items in the warehouse were typically found in such places: sealed crates of various sizes, some made of wood and others made of metal. On the right side was a brown door with a plaque containing the word 'office' printed in red capital letters.

The cashier parked the car next to the limousine and switched off the car ignition, and then we all stepped out.

Doctor Six stretch his arms high in the air, yawning as if he had just woken up. Chibi just stood by my side and looked around, stretching her own arms for no apparent reason. The cashier got out of the car last. She was dressed in what looked like a pseudo-police uniform (complete with a police beret and a forged police badge on the left side of the chest of her uniform) instead of the petrol station cashier uniform I saw her wear before.

She walked over and extended her hand to me, and said, "Hello, how are you? You remember me, don't you?"

I shook her hand and replied, "Yes, you were the cashier from that old petrol station. Are you part of our company as well?"

The cashier smiled and said, "Yeah, I am part of it. My name is Shaffa, and yours?"

"Omar," I replied.

Doctor Six stood next to me, his hand on my shoulder, and said to Shaffa, "But Omar's name will change to a nickname as soon as Face arrives."

There was a sound of a doorknob clicking, followed by the creaking of a door opening. We all looked to the right where the sound was coming from, and I saw a man wearing a gray trench coat and a fedora hat exit from the warehouse office. It was our manager Face!

"Hello, everyone!" Face chimed merrily. "I was informed that you all completed the mission. Now that neighborhood gang will finally be behind bars. Well done!"

We all smiled after Face had congratulated us. He walked up to me and warmly gave me a hug. When he let go of me, he told me, "Okay, Omar, since you passed this mission successfully, I will now dub you an official company nickname that will replace your real name. Are you ready for the change?" I replied to him without hesitation, "Yes, I am fully ready for my nickname to be put in place of my real name."

Face then said, "Alright then everyone, please stand at my sides for this important moment."

Shaffa, Doctor Six, and Chibi obediently stood next to Face, with the doctor at his right, and Shaffa and Chibi to his left respectively. All four of them were now facing me, while I stood still in front of them. Face began, "From this day forth, our newest employee Omar shall be nicknamed 'The Third One,' or 'Third One' for short. He will be addressed by this name from this day, as long as he continues to be a part of our company. Should he quit from our company for any reason, his nickname will be revoked and he will have his normal name again, and his company credentials will also be revoked. But I truly hope that he remains with us, for our company greatly cares for each and every one of its employees just as much as a family cares about each and every one of its relatives."

Face reached into his trench coat, pulled out a scroll wrapped in a red ribbon, and gave it to me. "This is your certificate in honor of your newfound position in our company. It previously belonged to an employee who had sadly passed away. He was the first employee to be named 'The Third One.' I felt that only a special newcomer with an equally good heart and persona deserved to have this title in our company, and you will be the one who will take his place and carry on his short-lived but promising legacy. Best of luck to you…Third One."

After Face's formal speech, everyone, including Face himself, clapped their hands. Even Chibi, whose hands only made soft patting sounds, clapped for me as loudly as she could. I felt tears brimming in my eyes. I felt very happy inside, even happier than when I celebrated my university graduation with my family in my previous normal life. From this moment, the company was now my new family, just as 'The Third One' was now my new name. Unable to contain myself in this joyous moment, the tears in my eyes slowly flowed down my cheeks.

"Thank you, everybody," I said when everyone finally stopped clapping. "I will do my best in the company, and I have no thoughts about leaving it at all."

Then Face exclaimed, "That's the spirit, kid! Now go with Shaffa and the other two, they will take you back to company headquarters so that you can start writing your report on this mission. And after you're done with the report, one of the staff members will come into your room tomorrow and take the report to me, so that I can evaluate it and then add it to the company archives. I'll be staying here for a while longer; got to make some important phone calls. See you later, Third One!" Face walked back towards the office in the warehouse, and closed the door behind him. I followed the others towards the row of parked vehicles.

Shaffa took out a bunch of car keys from her pocket, picked one, and then put the other keys back. She pressed a button on the key to electronically unlock the doors of the white limousine with black tinted windows. She opened the driver's side door and got in. Doctor Six opened the right rear door of the long limo and told me, "Hop in, Third One." I got in, saw Chibi swiftly jump in and sit next to me, and then finally Doctor Six got inside and closed the door. I heard Shaffa start the engine, and after a few seconds, we were out of the warehouse and back on the road.

The interior of the limousine was pretty high-class, as expected. Red and blue neon lights illuminated the ceiling, and a little table with snacks and drinks was fixed in front of the seats we were sitting on. Other passenger seats lay at the very front of us past the table, right behind the barrier that separated the driver from backseat passenger area. Doctor Six poured some orange juice into a fancy glass, and handed it to me. As I took a sip from the deliciously fresh-tasting orange juice, Doctor Six said to me, "Congratulations again, Third One. I am glad that you are now a permanent member of our company. We will support you at all times when you're in need, and you can do the same for us in the future once you gain more experience."

I replied, "Thanks, Doctor. I will do my best in the company."

We ate snacks and talked about other things en route to my office, things that I did not remember. When I arrived, Doctor Six led me to my room and reminded me to write the report. I set up the laptop computer and typed up the report. After completing the report, I fell asleep.

Letter

I woke up the next morning with my head buried in my crossed arms on the desk. I noticed the computer was still on, with the last page of my report still shown on the screen. I remembered that I worked on typing the report yesterday evening, and then after finishing it I lay my head on the desk to rest for a little bit. Unsurprisingly, I had fallen fast asleep all the way until this morning.

I reached for the opened suitcase on my desk that had been given to me for my job, and took out a small, blue-colored USB storage device. I plugged the device in one of the three USB ports on my laptop computer, saved, and closed the file containing the report, copied the file to the device, and then I removed the USB device and set it on the desk. I was going to turn off my computer when I heard a recognizable beeping sound in my pocket. It was my mobile phone which I had not used since the day I first walked into the company building.

I pulled out my phone and looked at its screen. The battery was almost dead, which explained the beeping sound. But something was not right: why hadn't I received any calls from anyone? I usually get at least one or two phone calls every day, but ever since joining this company I apparently did not get any calls. My parents did not even call me; they always called me on my cell phone whenever I was gone from the house for more than five hours, just to make sure that I was all right at wherever I was. It's almost as if everyone whom I had known before had forgotten about me.

I looked around my office to find a phone charging station. As expected, there was indeed an area in the room where I could charge up my phone: Fixed against the wall next to the desk was a rectangular plug port with six protruding wires, each of which were compatible with many cell phones. I picked the wire charger that matched my phone port, and then plugged my phone in to charge.

I tried dialing my house number from my phone while it was charging. I heard ringing on the other end. Three rings. Four rings. Five. Six. Seven. Then no response. I hung up, then decided to dial my mother's number. I heard a mechanical robot voice tell me that the mobile phone I was trying to call was either switched off or outside the designated calling area. I hung up again and tried calling my father. I had the same response as before. I hung up and tilted my head back on the chair, thinking about my situation.

Then I suddenly felt sad inside. I had missed my sister Noora's birthday, and the gift that I had bought for her was alive and already owned as one of this company's precious employees! I wondered how Noora was coping with me being gone from the house. She probably cried her eyes out upon knowing that I was not at home after the first day of my employment with the company.

I forcibly shook my head to shake off my sadness, and while thinking more clearly I realized that I had worn the same clothes for more than a day! I decided it was best to take a shower right after I ate breakfast, before I get a call to participate in another mission. I went to the kitchen and quickly poured myself a bowl of cereal for breakfast, and ate. After eating my breakfast, I remembered something: I had no spare clothes with me. Upon being immediately accepted into this company on the same day as meeting with its manager, I had not anticipated living with the company directly after being accepted; therefore, I did not have any extra clothes readily packed. So I walked back to the main part of my office to call Face about providing some clothes to me.

I froze in my place: I saw a young woman wearing a business suit sitting on my desk chair. When she saw me, she got up from the chair and said in a polite British accent, "Hello there, Third One! I am sorry to intrude, but I wanted to tell you some important information. Do you remember me? I am the receptionist from downstairs." After she had said that, I instantly recognized her: she was the receptionist I had spoken to when I first set foot in the company building.

"Yes, I remember you," I replied, "you were the one who told me to meet with the manager Face the first time I arrived here."

The receptionist smiled, extended her hand, and said, "My name is Helen, I am the receptionist of Ruof Researchers Corporation. Again, I apologize for my unexpected intrusion." I shook her hand lightly, then let go. She sat back down and patted the second desk chair with her hand. "Please sit down, Third One. There are a few things that I must tell you." I sat down and listened to her.

"Our company noticed that you had tried to contact your parents earlier." My eyes widened upon hearing this, and I looked at the ceiling to see if there were any surveillance cameras visible. Helen then said, "Do not worry; there are no cameras in this room. Your phone, however, is tapped for security purposes, and all numbers dialed, as well as all incoming and outgoing calls, are recorded."

I thought about what she said for a moment and realized I should have known about the phone being tapped. After all, this is a highly confidential company, so it was plainly fitting that calls and numbers dialed would be recorded for security reasons. But still, how did the company know about my mobile phone number beforehand to get it tapped for surveillance? They must have been observing me for longer than I imagined!

Helen continued, "Anyway, one of the reasons why I was sent here by Face was to tell you that your parents, upon hearing that you had acquired a job, had moved out of the country this morning, taking along with them your sister Noora."

I felt a twinge of sharpness jab at my heart. Did this mean that my parents did not care about me, that they raised me until I became an adult and then left me by myself? "Which…country did they move to?" I asked slowly, my voice hinting of sadness.

Helen replied, "They moved to the United States. They had taken the flight to the States yesterday, but we do not know exactly where in the States they had travelled to. However, your mother did tell us to give you a message." She reached into her blazer pocket and took out a crumpled piece of white paper. She opened it up and gave it to me.

It was a note written in blue ink by my mother in her own cursive handwriting. I felt a jolt of great sorrow as I read it silently:

Dear Omar,

Congratulations on finally getting a job, my dear son. I am very happy for you, and your sister Noora is also happy for you. But your father's reaction was very strange, he did not seem very happy. He shouted at the member of your company who told us about the good news, telling him that he did not like the idea of you working and living in a company that isn't well-known. But he said that he hopes you would make enough money for yourself so that you can have a good future. Your father and sister and I will move to the US tomorrow, we will be traveling tomorrow morning. We are moving away because we knew you will be able to live on your own now that you have a good job, even though your father did not really approve of it. We agreed that we wanted you to see how it feels to be on your own. Noora cried when she heard we were all leaving without you, but don't worry about anything. The company member gave us your office contact number and email address, so that we can talk to you once in a while. And we still have your mobile number so don't ever change it. We will never come back to see you again, but we will keep in touch by phone calls and emails. I wish you all the best in your job, my son!

Sincerely,
Your Mother

I closed my eyes, clenched my teeth, and closed my hand into a fist to crush the paper. I could feel tears building up behind my eyelids; eventually the tears flowed out and I sobbed lightly. I opened my eyes and saw that Helen, keeping her own composure, offered me some tissues. I took the tissues, wiped my tears from my face, and blew my nose as quietly as I could. "Shall I continue, Third One?" Helen asked politely, her expression still the same since she barged in. I nodded, took a deep breath, and leaned back on my seat to relax myself. Helen went on, "Do not be sad, Third One. The company had arranged to seal off your parents' house so that no one tries to buy it or steal any of its contents. In addition, your personal belongings have been transported to one of our many warehouses that exist in the country, so that you can request any items you want transported here. And your wardrobe should arrive here at any second now."

At that moment, my office door opened and I saw Chibi walk inside, holding a huge cardboard box above her head. *Such a strong doll,* I thought amusingly. I smiled and waved at Chibi, trying to conceal the fact that I had cried earlier.

"Hi, Third One!" Chibi addressed joyfully. "Nothing like a little exercise in the morning to help me build up my arm muscles!" I laughed out loud when she said that, and Helen smiled. Chibi then asked, "So where should I set this box down? It's getting a little heavy." I motioned with my hand to the middle of the room, and she set it down there.

"Thanks, Chibi," I said to her.

Chibi replied, "No problem, Third One! Just doing my job." Then she walked out of the room, and the door automatically closed behind her.

Helen spoke again, "That box contains all your clothes from your house. Do not worry about where to store them; a proper closet to put your clothes in will be delivered here later today."

I looked at the box again and saw that it was sealed shut with clear tape. I looked around the room for something to cut the tape, and found some big scissors from inside the desk drawer. As I walked over to the box to open it, Helen grasped my hand and said quickly, "Wait, Mister Third One."

I looked at her and saw her pull out a wad of paper money from her pocket. She handed it to me and told me, "Based on your performance observed by Doctor Six and Chibi at the time of your first mission with them, Face has decided that this is your first salary amount."

My jaw dropped at the amount of money I held in my hand. This was an excellent starting salary for me!

Helen smiled after seeing my reaction. "Face is very generous to his employees," she said, "he tends to surprise them by giving them more than what they expect. My first salary was very high as well."

I stowed the money in a safe located in my desk drawer. Face was indeed very generous, I thought. I could not imagine what my next salary would be. I was very lucky to be favored by this company; I never would have thought I would get paid this much in the beginning of my work. This company was indeed very charitable towards its employees.

Helen said to me, "Your next salary will be awarded to you upon completion of the upcoming mission. Face may raise your next salary if he sees any major improvement in your performance."

"Thank you, Helen," I kindly said, and then I asked her, "Can you please send Face my thanks?"

"Yes, of course I will, Third One," said Helen. She got up from the chair and started walking towards the door, but then she stopped and turned around to face me again. She asked me, "By the way, do you still have the red pass slip I gave to you when you were first going to meet Face?"

I remembered that she had given it to me so that I would have permission to get to Face's office, although I did not need it at all the last time I met him. I stood up, took it out of my pocket, and showed it to her in my open hand. "Here it is, but I didn't need it," I said.

She walked to me, took the tiny red paper slip from my hand, and said, "Thank you for keeping it and not throwing it away later like most people would have done. This red paper is very special to me; I will tell you more about it whenever the next mission begins. Face stated that you will be joining me in the next mission."

I nodded my head. Just then, I heard a ring tone from a mobile phone that was not mine. Helen took out her cell phone from her pocket and answered it. She had a little conversation with the person on the other end, and just before the conversation ended, I heard her say, "Also, The Third One thanks you for his first salary…alright, I will tell him that…goodbye." Helen hung up the phone and told me, "That was Face. He told me to let you know that the next mission begins today, so please take your shower now, and get ready. Face says that you should put on something casual, and not wear anything fancy for this mission. I will be waiting for you downstairs at the reception area."

"Okay, Helen, I will be ready in a few minutes," I said to her.

Helen looked at the surface of my desk and noticed the blue USB storage stick which contained my first report. She picked up the USB stick and said, "Face told me that your report would be saved in this USB. I am sure you already saved a copy in it?" I nodded to her, confirming. "Alright then," Helen said, "see you downstairs!"

She put the USB device in her pocket, got up, and exited my office. After the door automatically closed, I used the heavy duty scissors that I found from my desk drawer to cut open the taped box and get some of my casual clothes. Then I went to the bathroom to take a shower in order to get ready for my next mission.

Interlude II

I woke up. I slept for nine hours.

I decided to sleep for the night in the shack, since I needed to give myself a break from writing my story. Fortunately, there was an old fashioned yet comfortable bed in this shack, right next to the table and chair which I made use of to write my story last night. I had woken up and ate my breakfast; I had with me a small backpack which held food that was prepared by Chibi, some of which consisted of a cheese sandwich and a blueberry muffin as my breakfast meal, and a bag of chocolate chip cookies as my snack.

Not exactly a big breakfast, but it will suffice for today. I must keep in mind that I have to finish writing my story in four more days at most, and then wait for one my colleagues to show up and collect the book containing my story. Shaffa will most probably be the one to come here and take the book, since she is usually the driver of the company. Helen may also tag along with her to pay me a visit.

In any case, the person who will be delivering my story to Face will be highly paid. The delivery of my story was a high priority mission, and I was determined to finish it in time so as not to delay the person coming to pick it up. In addition, the person coming here will give me hints to the direction of *it* so that I can continue my search.

Now, as of this page, I am sitting down again and continuing with writing my story. It is about nine o'clock in the morning; I have plenty of time until an employee gets here to collect my story. I shall write on…

Helen

I got ready and went downstairs to the reception area of the company building. I saw Helen, wearing a white lab coat over her suit, waiting for me. "Sorry I'm late," I apologized.

Helen replied, "Don't worry about it. Now let's go outside." We both walked outside the building.

The parking lot was virtually empty with the exception of one vehicle, as usual. I'm beginning to see a pattern here, I thought. Judging by the blankness of this place, no one really seemed to know or care about this company or this area as a whole. Or perhaps people avoided coming to this place simply due to its mysterious yet frighteningly vacant nature. Either way, this place was very free and surpassed the boundaries set by the conventions of everyday life.

The ambulance I saw from the warehouse the previous day was now parked in the handicap parking space. But this time appropriate emergency markings were painted on it, complete with license plates which were obviously forged.

"Emergency vehicles have the authority to park wherever they want to," chimed Helen. She took the key out of her pocket (I was expecting Chibi to be the key chain again, but this time there was a regular mini crystal-ball key chain attached to the key) and unlocked the door of the ambulance.

She stepped into the driver's seat, and I in the passenger's seat. She picked up a medical identification clip from the dashboard, and wore it on her lab coat. Then she started the engine, reversed, and drove out of the parking area.

"So Helen," I began politely, "can you please explain the significance of the little red piece of paper?" She glanced at me, probably surprised at my extremely polite way of speaking, and then looked back to the road. She said, "That red piece of paper was originally a part of a children's storybook. That book belonged to—"

"You?" I interjected quickly.

Helen sternly said, "No, the book did not belong to me, Third One. You must bear with me in order to understand the significance of the paper. Don't say anything until I finish."

"Sorry," I apologized.

Then Helen continued, "The children's storybook belonged to a little girl who had passed away in a burning house five years ago. She was an only child living in this house in the middle of the woods in the United States. Her mother and father were originally from Osaka, Japan, but they migrated to and lived in the United States. They all lived happily in a house somewhere in the Midwestern part of the States. At that time, I was babysitting the girl. I was eighteen years old and I needed the money to support myself in college, considering my parents sent me alone to America to study business administration. But that's another story which I may or may not tell you about in the future.

"Anyway, one day, while babysitting the little girl in her room, I heard shouting voices coming from the living room. Since I was babysitting the girl, her parents had gone from the house and therefore those voices were not of her parents. So I told the girl to wait in her room, and I had run downstairs to the living room. I saw two men; one was a fat man and the other a thin man. The fat man was holding a flask, and the thin man was holding a stick lit with fire – a torch. The fat man was shouting out orders to the thin man, urging him to throw the torch on the floor. As the fat one was shouting, he directed with his finger exactly where to toss the torch: Onto a spot on the carpet floor that was dampened with…petrol. I could tell it was petrol because of the strong smell.

"At first the two men didn't notice that I was in the room, but when I lunged for the thin man, the fat one took notice and simply stepped in front of me. I hit the fat man instead but his stance was too strong to be broken; he still stood while my face was buried in his stomach. With his free hand, he pushed me to the floor, and then dumped the liquid from the flask onto my body. The liquid that he poured on me was petrol. After that, the fat man shouted for the last time to the thin one to drop the torch, and he finally did that. The torch instantly set the moist section of the floor ablaze."

Helen stopped talking for a moment. I could see in her facial expression that she was preparing to tell me about a part of the story that was difficult for her to cope with. Although I was feeling shocked from all that she had said so far, I remained silent to let her mentally gather herself together. Then after about thirty seconds, without taking her eyes off the road, she continued:

"After the thin man dropped the torch on the floor, both men ran outside the front door, not closing the door behind them. The fire had spread throughout the room very quickly, and was trailing towards me. Since I still had the petrol on my clothes, there was a big chance that the fire would touch me and then I would be engulfed in flames. So I ran outside before the fire got to the front door. But then, I suddenly remembered that I had left the little girl in her room in the burning house. I was very naïve at the time, too naïve…"

Helen stopped again, and I saw tears form in her eyes and stream down her cheeks. She pulled a tissue from the lab coat pocket and used it to soak up the tears. Once again, I had given her some extra time to explain the story. Then she went on:

"So then I ran back inside the house, not caring if I got burned by the flames. I was very determined to get the little girl out of the house. My clothes had caught fire but I kept on running upstairs to the little girl's room. I opened the door and saw that she was busy reading one of her storybooks, somehow unaware of the house burning down. She looked up and began crying when she saw me, presumably because I was covered in flames. I told her – no, I screamed at her – to follow me, but my plea only made her cry more. Not thinking about the consequences of my actions, I ran up to her, picked her up while she was still holding on to her storybook, and ran downstairs to exit the house.

"After getting out of the burning house and into the grassy field, I quickly dropped and rolled the girl's body all over the ground first, then my own body. Eventually the fires on my body were extinguished, but I was in great pain. My clothes had mostly burned away, baring my burned skin. I looked at the girl and saw that she had been all right, but she had begun changing; she was actually shrinking before my very eyes. She shrunk to the size of my palm, and she looked slightly different. She was still clutching what was left of her storybook, which was now only a small piece of slightly rectangular red paper blackened on one of its sides. I took the red paper from her hand and looked at it. I cried for a very long time until emergency services eventually arrived. I had taken the girl and the slip of paper in my hand while I was laid down on a medical stretcher and put into an ambulance.

"I fell unconscious for some moments, but when I regained consciousness I saw that the vehicle transporting me was in fact not an ambulance, nor were the people taking care of me doctors." Helen glanced at me, looked back to the road, and said, "They were a strange yet friendly set of people. They were my saviors and the little girl's saviors. They were members of this very company that we are currently working in. They had hired me and the little girl to join their ranks in order to fight evil. I was given the nickname 'Helen,' and the little girl was nicknamed—"

"Chibi?" I interrupted. I could not stop myself from completing her sentence, as at this stage in her story the identity of the little girl was very obvious. Helen probably thought so as well, because she did not complain to me about my interrupting her.

"Yes," she said, "the little girl was nicknamed Chibi. To this day, she does not know of her past or how she transformed into a doll. And the company has made very clear to its members that no one should mention to Chibi anything about her past. The Chibi who you see now is the brightest and most cheerful member of the company, and this company aims to keep her that way. So please, Mister Third One, do not mention to Chibi any of what I told you so far."

"You have my word," I promised Helen.

She looked at me, smiled, and said, "Thank you, Mister Third One. You are a very kind and thoughtful young man. I knew deep inside that you were a good person when I entrusted you with the red paper on that day." I smiled back and nodded to her in shy agreement.

Helen rolled up the left sleeve of her white lab coat and looked at her watch, then exclaimed, "Oh my goodness, we will be late for the mission if we don't go faster!" She switched on the emergency sirens in a successful attempt to make the other vehicles in front of us move out of the way, and then she pressed harder on the accelerator to speed up to the location of the second mission.

Accident

Helen sped and swerved through the streets until we reached heavy traffic and came to a stop. She increased the volume of the ambulance sirens, but it was no use; the traffic ahead of us was at a standstill. I heard the engine of the ambulance switch off. I looked to the driver's side and saw that Helen had switched off the engine and taken the key out of its ignition slot. "What are you doing?" I asked her.

She handed me a walkie-talkie that was apparently stowed inside the center storage console next to the armrest, and then said, "Listen to me very carefully, Mister Third One. Since I cannot get us through the traffic in the ambulance, I need you to run to the scene of the accident on foot. In this mission, we must rescue the victims of the accident up ahead. The accident is only a few blocks down the road; you can reach it in time if you run fast enough."

"And what about you? What will you do?" I asked her, feeling nervous. I felt beads of sweat forming across my forehead.

She said, "Don't worry about me, Mister Third One; I will catch up to you. I must give Face a call to inform him about this situation. Besides, I do not think it is a good idea for me to abandon the ambulance, since the people around us may become suspicious about an unoccupied emergency vehicle stopped in the middle of the traffic. Now go on ahead, Mister Third. I will be fine."

I nodded, got out of the ambulance, and ran as quickly as possible past the stopped cars, gripping the walkie-talkie tightly in my right hand. As I ran, I heard impatient drivers rapidly honking their car horns in failed attempts to force the cars in front to start moving. I ignored the annoying sounds of the car horns and concentrated on getting to the scene of the accident.

Within less than a minute, I finally arrived at the place of the accident. My eyes widened as I saw just how bad this accident was. A dirty white semi-truck had overturned on its left side, its massive rectangular container trailer crushing two compact cars that were on its left. A huge crowd of people was gathered around the accident, some of them using their mobile phones to either take snapshots or record videos of the catastrophe. I did not see any emergency vehicles at the scene; the massive traffic jam likely prevented police and medical vehicles from getting to the accident.

Suddenly, amidst the loud honking of the car horns and confused shouts of people, I heard Helen's voice coming from my walkie-talkie, "Mister Third One, how many victims are there in the accident?" I looked at the cockpit of the white overturned truck and saw no one in there, but I saw a man and a woman stuck inside one of the crushed compact cars. The man, who was sitting in the driver's seat, was pounding his fists on the cracked driver's side window of the car in an effort to break the window and escape the wreckage. His door looked like it was mangled out of shape from the accident, so the man was not able to open the door.

No other person was in any of the other vehicles involved in the accident; presumably, those who were initially in those vehicles had not been injured and had escaped to safety somewhere in the immense crowd, waiting for emergency vehicles to show up. I wondered whether those people initially tried to save the trapped couple, or if they simply ignored them and were only concerned about their own safety. Either way, it was I who would take the initiative to rescue the couple.

"I see two victims in the accident, a man and a woman, stuck in their car," I replied to Helen through the walkie-talkie. "The man has a little cut on his forehead, and he's trying to break the driver's side window to get out of the car. The driver's side door is crooked because of the accident, so the man can't open the door. The lock that is holding the door shut is probably jammed from the inside."

I waited for Helen's response for a few seconds, then she said, "Alright, Third One, try to find something strong enough to break the glass of the driver's side window, but take caution while doing so as to not hurt the two people by mistake. And after you rescue them, wait for me to get there."

"Okay, I'll be careful," I replied to Helen.

I set my walkie-talkie down on the road and looked around frantically for something that would be strong enough to break the window of the half-crushed compact car. A circular metallic lid that covered a sewer drain was a few steps in front of me. I walked over and found that the lid was slightly opened. I tried will all my strength to pull the lid free, and I succeeded. It was pretty heavy and strong, perfect for breaking the window. I carried the slightly rusted sewer lid with me to the car, and once I got there, the man stopped hammering his fists on the window. His facial expression turned from terror to relief when he saw me. His female partner had also looked happy to see me. I shouted to them as loud as I could, "Move away from the window!" The couple had heard my order and moved as far away from the driver's side window as they possibly could. Then I lifted the sewer lid up with both hands and then thrust it into the window as hard as I could.

Most of the window shattered, with some parts of the window still left. I broke the rest of the window using the lid in order to get rid of the jagged parts that may hurt the two people on their way out. Slowly and carefully, they climbed out of their car, avoiding the broken glass. The man immediately gave me a big hug and thanked me for my help. The woman also thanked me, tears of joy trickling down her eyes.

I heard the sound of a motorcycle coming to our direction. And sure enough, in the distance I saw a red motorcycle driving towards us, steadily snaking its way through the traffic jam. The motorcycle rider, whom I did not recognize, parked a few steps away from us, jumped off of the motorcycle, and walked over to us. The rider wore a full black leather outfit resembling that of motorcycle race drivers, complete with a shiny motorcycle helmet. The person took the helmet off, and I saw long blonde hair appear from the back of the person's head. It was Helen. She took a small white container out of her pocket. "Are these two hurt anywhere?" she asked.

"The man just has a little cut on his forehead," I replied, gesturing at the man that I rescued. Hearing this, she quickly set her helmet down on the ground, walked over to the man, took out a gauze and bandage from the container, and secured them on the man's forehead to seal up the wound.

The people from the big crowd clapped and cheered happily in our direction, with most of them aiming their phone cameras at us to snap photos and record video footage of the scene. I saw Helen smiling and waving at them, and I did the same. I felt like I had accomplished something big; this was the first time I had rescued total strangers from danger. Before joining the company, the only life I had saved was that of a friend rather than someone I didn't know. I recalled the one time when my friend Mark was about to be knifed by a delinquent school student over a simple argument about a video game, but then I quickly interjected and talked things over with that student. Eventually, I prevented Mark from being seriously injured by the student, and that student had left him alone since then. It was true that I had saved Mark from danger, but he was a person that I had known personally, and I usually only cared the most about people that I knew well. The man and woman I saved were complete strangers, yet I had managed to look past the fact that they were strangers and pushed myself to save them from injury or death anyway. Regardless of whether or not the accident happened to be a part of the mission, I would still stand by my feelings that I needed to rescue them.

The clapping and cheering from the crowd of people had suddenly stopped short. With the noisy sounds from the masses of people now minimized, I heard the repetitive hums of a helicopter propeller nearing closer to the area we were in. Everyone, including me, looked up towards the skies, searching for the flying helicopter. Then, appearing from behind a building right next to the accident scene was a vanilla white helicopter with some sort of cylindrical tank beneath it. It flew about two stories above us, which was dangerously close considering that the accident was in an area surrounded by many buildings close together.

Helen and I ducked to avoid hazardous contact with the helicopter should it come too close to us. The big crowd of people had also done the same; some of them even dove to the ground in haste as the helicopter hovered lower and lower. A few others stood their ground recording the helicopter with their cell phone cameras. While crouching, I looked to my left and saw that Helen had walked back to her bike. Was she going to intentionally leave me here in the middle of possible danger?

I realized that she was taking something out of the cube-shaped storage compartment attached behind the motorcycle. She lifted the lid, took out two gas masks, walked back over to me and handed me one of the masks. "Put this on, Mister Third One," she ordered. I did what she told me to do, and she put on her mask after I did. I wanted to ask her if we should warn the people about something dangerous about to happen, but it was too late. I heard a long sharp hiss coming from the helicopter, and saw some dark green smoke spraying out of a small outlet below the helicopter's tank, towards the mass of people.

Some people screamed and tried to run away from the smoke, but within seconds, it drifted quickly throughout the area, covering the city blocks as far as where Helen's ambulance was parked. One by one, two by two, and three by three, the people around me (including the couple I had assisted earlier), coughed rapidly upon inhaling the gas, and eventually they all fell to the ground unconscious. Most of the people whom were waiting in their cars in the traffic jam had stared in horror as people fell down unconscious in front of their eyes, some pointing their phone cameras our direction to record video footage of what was happening. A few other people foolishly got out of their cars and tried running away, but the drifting smoke easily got to their lungs, and they fell down just like the big crowd of pedestrians before them. I looked up at the buildings around the area and saw people staring outside their apartment windows, sheer terror on their faces at the sight of the chaos outside and of the continuously swelling cloud of dark green smoke.

I did not like what I saw happening around me. I grabbed Helen's arm and shouted angrily, "What are you doing? Call Face quick, we need reinforcements!"

But Helen pulled away from my grip and told me, "No, Mister Third One, everything is under control. Look." She pointed to the helicopter, and I saw that it had landed on the road. I could not see who was inside the helicopter due to its windows being darkly tinted, but when the door of the helicopter opened, I saw its occupants.

Doctor Six was the one who opened the door, and Shaffa was the helicopter pilot.

"Get in, you two!" Doctor Six ordered loudly in the midst of the noisy sounds of the helicopter propeller and screaming people. Helen and I ran to the helicopter, and Doctor Six pulled me inside first, then Helen. He closed the door and told Shaffa to hover back into the air. As we elevated above the buildings, I could see that the cloud of smoke became so thick that I could not see through it anymore. The smoke had completely covered the area of the accident, and the ends of the huge smoke cloud had extended further into other neighboring vicinities.

I felt very angry inside. I could not believe that Doctor Six and Shaffa were responsible for the chaos that gripped the area of the accident. They had knocked out dozens of people with the chemical smoke, and now the place was filled not only with stationary vehicles, but also with fainted people scattered all over the places the smoke had touched.

"So what was that all about?" I shouted furiously at Doctor Six. "Those people were innocent, you had no right to do that to them!"

Doctor Six frowned and sharply replied to me, "Those people down there were not completely innocent. Did you not see that they had not tried to rescue the two people from the accident? All they did was stand there and watch as the couple was trying to get out of their car. Not one person in that crowd wanted to save them; they simply stood there and watched while the people inside were slowly suffering in panic."

"But those people didn't try to rescue them because they were waiting for the proper authorities to show up," I argued. "They had no choice but to wait—"

"Shaffa? Please land here for one moment," Doctor Six ordered, cutting me off. I felt the helicopter steadily descend. I looked out the window and saw that Shaffa was obediently landing the helicopter on the rooftop of a tall building. Once we landed, Doctor Six opened the door and stepped outside. "Third, please get out and come with me," Doctor Six ordered, "and Shaffa, keep the chopper running. We will be back; I just want to explain something to Third One."

I got out of the helicopter and walked up to Doctor Six. I stood in front of him and saw his arms extend slowly. Then suddenly, he grabbed the front of my shirt with both his hands and dragged me towards the edge of the rooftop. I was so shocked from the doctor's sudden violent reaction that I only put my own hands on his arms in a feeble attempt to calm him down. I did not try to resist his grip on me.

He held me right next to the edge of the roof. I turned my head and looked down through the corner of my right eye. The building we were on was very high; there would be no way to survive a fall to the ground from this height. And I felt a quick but strong wind push against me, as if it was silently helping the doctor throw me off the roof. I felt a rush of fear seep through me.

I turned my head back to face the doctor's white pupilless eyes. "All right Third One," the doctor began, "what are you going to do now? Are you going to wait for your fellow staff members to rescue you, or are you going to take action?"

I looked past the doctor's menacing face and saw that Helen and Shaffa had been staring at us from the helicopter. Neither had moved nor said a word to each other. They just sat in there and watched, just like the big crowd of people that were gathered at the scene of the accident.

I pushed the doctor with all my might and succeeded in pushing him away from me, but I had lost my balance and was about to fall off the edge of the rooftop. Thankfully, at that very moment, Doctor Six grabbed my right hand with both his hands and quickly pulled me up to the safety away from the edge. I wobbled awkwardly in order to stand up straight, and looked at him. He smiled and said to me, "Now do you understand? Just now, you had countered the problem yourself instead of waiting for help to arrive, and as a result, you managed to save a life. Your own life, that is."

He pointed at the helicopter, at Shaffa and Helen, and then said, "As you can see, those two merely sat and watched as I was going to throw you off the roof. They were purposely acting like the cowardly people that were grouped at the accident scene. They did not even try to save you, most likely because they were afraid of my possessing more power and authority than them. But you were not afraid to push me away, even though you knew that I was ranked higher than you in the company."

I thought about what Doctor Six had said to me, and decided that he was right. It was better to take matters into my own hands, rather than idly waiting for someone else to assist me, when the time was right to do so. Still, I told him, "But I still don't think the people watching the accident deserved what you and Shaffa did to them. They had no idea what to do about the situation."

Doctor Six's face became expressionless as he became silent for some moments. Then he finally responded, "You know, Third One, you are absolutely correct about one thing. Those people did not know what to do. But that is exactly what I am getting at here. Don't you see? Those people should have had some common sense. They should know that when others are in trouble, and when they witness the trouble first-hand, they should take responsibility as fellow human beings to save one another. It's a very logical state-of-mind that many people nowadays just do not seem to understand. Everybody is afraid of saving one another because they are afraid of taking the responsibility of saving one another. This fear of being responsible should be erased so that people can have the confidence to save one another from danger, and eventually start caring about one another."

I looked down to the surface of the rooftop in stillness, thinking about Doctor Six's wise speech. Then I looked at him again when he continued, "And the idea of spraying sleeping gas on the people was my idea; Shaffa had nothing to do with it. I am the one who decided on the idea because it was the only way to punish those people for their light crimes without hurting them physically. One of the rules we must follow as members of this company is that we mustn't harm any innocent person. However, we are required to apply disciplinary measures wherever needed in our ongoing quests to reduce evil in the world."

Doctor Six at last motioned with his hand for me to come with him back to the helicopter. I walked next to him and asked him, "Will those people be okay?"

The doctor replied, "Yes, they will be all right. The sleeping gas sprayed on them consists of a very weak chemical compound that does not have long-lasting effects, so the people should wake up in" – he looked at his watch – "five minutes from now." He put his hand on my shoulder. "Don't worry, Third One. As a member of the company, I would never hurt an innocent person; doing so would mean I would have to resign from the company and choose a life of evil. I do not want any evil in my life."

We got back in the helicopter and flew away from the roof of the building. Helen told me that we were going back to company headquarters, since we had finished the mission. I was looking forward to taking a nice long nap as soon as I returned to my office. But the incident that would take place upon my arrival to company headquarters was something that I did not look forward to.

Dismissal

Shaffa landed the helicopter on the roof of our company building. We all stepped out of the helicopter, with Doctor Six leading the way to the roof outlet that allowed access to the floors below. When he opened the door of the outlet, he stopped and literally jumped back. Face had been standing in the open doorway, dressed in his trench coat and fedora despite the hot weather, his head pointing downwards. He slowly lifted his head up, and smiled. But the smile on his face did not seem very friendly this time; it was a rather malicious frown. His eyes stared at all of us with a conspicuous hostility.

Face then told Doctor Six, "Doctor, please come here." The doctor did as he was told, and suddenly Face punched him in the stomach. Doctor Six uttered a grunting sound, and held his stomach with both hands. Face then roughly pushed him to the ground with one hand. Doctor Six moaned in pain and shivered while on the ground, as if he had a light seizure. Face walked towards him until he reached the tips of the doctor's shoes.

"I am very disappointed in you, Doctor," Face began menacingly, "you attacked innocent people during the earlier mission. Why did you do that? You never did such a thing before."

"Those…people did not help the victims in the accident," Doctor Six croaked in reply. After hearing his response, Face kicked him hard in his side. Doctor Six let out another moan of pain.

Then Face said, "You are an idiot, Doctor. As far as you're concerned, you had no right to do anything to those people. Not a single one of them had any idea of what to do about the accident in the first place. It is not their fault that they didn't know what to do; they were never taught how to rescue people. Only the emergency services are trained to save people. Those people were average-minded pedestrians who didn't possess the willpower, knowledge and experience needed for rescuing others. Use your common sense, Doctor."

I was in truth very surprised at Face's reaction, but decided not to show it. I kept my cool, just as Helen and Shaffa did, in order to avoid confrontation.

Doctor Six, still lying on the ground clutching his stomach, said harshly, "Do people need to be…*taught* to rescue others? People should be able to save lives without having second thoughts." Now Doctor Six got up slowly from the ground, and pointed to me while still fixing his gaze at Face. "Take Third One, our newest member, for example. He did not have the knowledge or experience of emergency services, but he still had the determination to save the couple stuck in the car."

Face stood still, silent and motionless, his pale white face seeming to turn even paler. The doctor had a point, I thought. I was willing to save the man and the woman trapped in their car, even though I did not possess the qualifications of an emergency services specialist. True, I was forced by Helen as part of the mission to rescue the victims of the accident, but I would have refused and backed down had it not been for my own willingness to save them.

After a fairly long period of silence, Face finally replied to the doctor, "Third One is now a member of this company, so naturally he was already *authorized* to rescue them. The pedestrians watching the accident aftermath, on the other hand, did not have *any* authorization whatsoever to do anything. If anything, their duty was to simply witness the scenario and wait till help arrives. I rest my case."

Now I was really taken aback; I raised my eyebrows when I heard Face's unusually narrow-minded conclusion of the issue. The doctor was shocked as well; his eyes widened and his mouth opened slightly. Oppositely, Helen and Shaffa kept their facial expressions as lifeless as before; perhaps they were used to Face talking this way. Or perhaps they were simply following their manager's orders like the good employees that they were.

Face walked up to the doctor and snatched away the familiar identification card that was attached to the doctor's lab coat. "Doctor Six," Face began, "you are fired. You deliberately violated the company policy by harassing innocent civilians, and you foolishly tried to justify your horrible misconduct. From this day onwards, you will no longer be known as Doctor Six. You will now be addressed by your real name: Isaac Warren. Furthermore, your status and your profession in this company shall be taken away from you." Face threw the doctor's ID card on the ground and heavily stomped on it three times. The doctor, with the back of his right hand, wiped away the little droplets of tears that formed near the ends of his eyes. I never thought that I would ever see a man like Doctor Six (or Isaac Warren), as he is now officially known as cry in front of me. He didn't seem like a man who would let his emotions sway him in front of a crowd.

After he finished stomping the identity card, Face kicked it so hard that it flew up from the ground towards Helen's face, but with her quick reflexes, she caught the card with both her hands. "Helen, please make sure his ID card is completely disposed of," Face ordered, "I don't want any trace of it to be found anywhere." Helen nodded obediently. Then Face turned back to Isaac Warren and said to him, "I want you to leave the premises immediately; you know the way down and out of the building. And don't try anything funny; there are cameras everywhere in the halls, you know. And you won't be taking anything from your room; I had it electronically locked ever since hearing about the fiasco you caused today. Besides, the company needs to confiscate everything you have for records as per company policy. You are probably aware of that already." Face pointed to the doorway of the roof outlet, his cold gaze still fixed on Isaac, and then said severely, "Get out of here and don't come back again."

I watched as Isaac walked towards the doorway and then disappeared into the outlet. I felt very sad inside; the man who just walked away was pretty much a mentor to me ever since I joined the company. He taught me very well during my early stages working in the company, and he also provided me with interesting information on the activities of the company. And most of all, he saved me from being injured by a gang member during my first mission. I felt like I had lost a colleague which I had greatly trusted.

Once Isaac was gone from our sights, Face turned around towards us and said, "Alright, guys, time for you all to go back to your rooms and take a break for the rest of the day." Shaffa smiled and walked to the outlet. Helen had a worried look on her face. Face asked her, "What's wrong, Helen? Is something bothering you?"

She said, "Yes, Mister Face, I just remembered that we had left the company motorcycle behind."

I expected Face to shout at her angrily for her mistake, but instead he calmly told her, "Don't worry about that, Helen. You were wearing gloves during this mission, remember?" He pointed at her gloved hands, and then said, "Even though the police confiscated the bike by now, they will find no fingerprints on it, or any other evidence for that matter, because you wore a full leather outfit. I applaud you for your smart choice in attire for that part of the mission."

Helen smiled in relief. Then Face finally said, "Now you go on ahead, Helen. Forget about that motorcycle; it has been officially dismissed from the company just like Isaac was. I will find replacements for both of the dismissals, so don't you worry." After Face's bitter concluding statements, Helen went downstairs through the outlet.

I began following Helen, but then Face raised his hand and said, "Wait just a minute, Third One."

I stopped in my tracks and asked very politely, so as to not show any signs of uneasiness, "Yes, Face?"

He put his left hand on my shoulder, looked into my eyes, and then said, "I really appreciated what you did today in your second mission. You followed Helen's orders and flawlessly helped those in danger." He pulled his hand away from my shoulder and used it to pull out a wad of paper money from his trench coat pocket. "Here's your salary," he said while putting the bundle of cash in my hand. Then he quickly pulled out more money and slapped the thick stack onto the other one that rested in my open hand. "And here's a little extra. What you did today proves that you deserve much more now. Consider this a hefty bonus."

My eyes widened at the amount of money in my hand. This was a lot of money for me. At the rate I was going, I could become rich in just a matter of days!

But my eyes returned back to normal when I thought about Isaac Warren, the man formerly nicknamed as Doctor Six. I felt bad about him not being a part of the company anymore.

Face broke away my brief thought when he said, "Okay Third One, you can go now. Remember to write down the report of today's mission. One of my associates will collect the report from you tomorrow." With his permission, I walked past him towards the opened roof outlet. Before going downstairs, I looked back and saw him smiling at me with a toothy grin that did not match his usually friendly personality.

Newspaper

Upon completion of the report of my second mission, and upon eating a large dinner after that (which I had made on my own in my kitchen), I decided to sleep early for the night. I slept early because I wanted to stop thinking about what had happened to Isaac Warren, the man that was formerly known as Doctor Six. Trying to sleep in order to stop those thoughts was not an easy task; the thoughts kept coming back to me, minute after minute, until I was too tired to think about anything anymore. Eventually, I fell asleep heavily and dreamlessly.

Then I woke up the next morning, feeling fresh but still somewhat troubled by the events that happened the previous day. It was difficult for me to accept the fact that Doctor Six was no longer a part of the company. But I silently told myself that I would try to bear with his absence, and at the same time I hoped that Face would one day have a change of heart and allow Isaac to return to the company.

I got out of bed, ate cereal for breakfast, took a shower, got dressed in casual clothes, walked back to the main part of my office, and sat at my desk. I looked around my office, thinking about what to do to pass some time away while I waited for one of Face's associates to show up. I kept looking around the room, and straight away, my gaze fixed on the cardboard box that I had opened the day before. It still lay open on the floor in the middle of the room, containing my clothes that I had worn in the past when I had lived with my parents and younger sister. I got up and walked over to the box, and sat on the carpeted floor to get the clothes out of the box.

I dug into the box and pulled out each piece of clothing one at a time until the box was empty. I then arranged the clothes carefully; I piled shirts with shirts, trousers with trousers, and so on. Now all my clothes were properly arranged on the floor, albeit a little wrinkled due to being scrunched in the box for some time. I was suddenly reminded that I needed an ironing set so that I could iron my clothes to remove the wrinkles. As Helen promised, a closet was indeed delivered to my room (it stood against the wall right next to my bed) so that I could store my clothes in it. And there was already a washing machine and dryer machine in my bathroom so I could wash and dry my clothes. So all I needed now was an ironing set. I got up and walked to the phone to call Face so he can have it delivered to my room. Helen had told me the day before that I could request the delivery of any of my belongings, which she had said were all safely stowed away in one of the company's warehouses.

I picked up my desk phone and my thumb intuitively rested on the number buttons, ready to dial Face's office extension number. But then, I remembered that I did not know his number.

I set the phone down and quickly looked through my suitcase. There had to be some sort of notepad with a listing of the company's contact numbers written in it, or something similar. Sure enough, I found a little book with a red hardcover which had the words 'phone numbers' written on the cover in bold black font. I opened the book and saw many phone numbers. The very first phone number written on the first page of the book was Face's: His office number. And the numbers that followed were of other company members: Doctor Six (who was now officially expelled from the company), Chibi, Helen, Shaffa, and numerous other names that were unfamiliar to me. Everyone in the long list had both an office phone number and a cell phone number except for Face, who only had an office phone number shown. Even Chibi, surprisingly, had a cell phone number, despite her being about the size of a cell phone! Perhaps her cell phone was very tiny; I would have to ask her about it the next time I see her…

Chibi.

I suddenly remembered that she was not present yesterday afternoon, after my second mission was completed. The last time I saw her was yesterday morning when she brought my box of clothes into my office. Perhaps Face decided not to let her meet me and the others at the end of the mission because he didn't want her to witness the doctor's dismissal from the company. I imagine that if she was present at that time, her reaction would have been extremely depressing, since she seemed to be very close with Doctor Six. I wondered if Face had already told her about his firing the doctor from the company. I decided that I would ask him about Chibi over the phone, after I ask him about delivering my iron set.

I picked up my desk phone again and dialed Face's office number according to the number written in the phone book. I heard the phone ringing from the other end, then after three rings Face answered, "Hello?"

I hesitated for a second, and then I responded, "Hi Face, it's Third One."

Face said, "Hey Third One! How are you doing?"

I replied, "I'm doing okay. I just called to ask for an iron set to be delivered to my room, so that I could get rid of the wrinkles in my clothes."

Face then said, "Roger that, Third One! It will be delivered to you today as soon as possible. I'll tell one of my associates to bring it to your room. Is there anything else?"

I paused again, and then I said to him, "Yes, actually I wanted to ask you about something else. Does Chibi know that…Doctor Six is not with the company anymore? I was just curious because she didn't show up yesterday when our second mission was completed."

I heard Face clear his throat, and then he answered, "Yes, I told Chibi about that unfortunate circumstance just this morning. However, she didn't take the news very well; I had to call in reinforcements to keep her in order."

I shivered at the last few words that he had said. What did he mean by calling in 'reinforcements to keep her in order?' Did little Chibi, upon hearing of Doctor Six's removal from the company, cause enough commotion to alert Face to call in security forces in order to restrain her?

"But don't worry Third One, Chibi is okay," Face continued. "Our company forgives its employees for faults related to emotional trauma. She was only lightly punished, but now she is fine."

Angry feelings swept me all over. I could not believe that Face allowed Chibi to be punished, even if it was light punishment that was given to her. According to how Helen had described Chibi's past, Chibi had been through a lot and did not even remember what had happened in her life before she transformed into a doll. She had lost her house, her parents, and her humanity, and she miraculously changed into a doll with abilities that were clearly inhuman. I strongly opposed the idea of punishing her in any way.

Face broke my thoughts away when he continued further, "And Chibi didn't show up yesterday because she was undergoing a mission separate from yours. In fact, her mission was so lengthy that she returned to company headquarters late last night. Therefore I decided to tell her about the doctor's dismissal this morning; I didn't want to tell her about it last night because she looked very tired after completing her mission."

I thought for a second about what Face said. His explanation about why Chibi had not shown up at the end of my second mission sounded plausible, but I was still slightly in doubt because I felt that Face was only telling me a fraction of the truth. I did not trust him as much as I did when I first joined the company due to his prejudiced nature towards Doctor Six yesterday. Nevertheless, I contained myself while on the phone in order to avoid revealing my distrust to Face.

"Well then," I continued casually, "I'm glad to hear that Chibi is fine, she will probably get over Doctor Six's absence in no time."

"Yeah, I'm sure she will quickly get over his absence," Face assured. "Besides, there are plenty of other potential candidates to take on the role as the company doctor. A replacement will be in order soon. Anything else you would like to ask me, Third One?"

"Nope," I replied easily. "that's all."

"Okay then, Third One," Face said, "your ironing set shall be delivered to your office real soon. Talk to you later!"

"Bye," I concluded.

I heard a click on the other end, meaning that Face had hung up.

I set the phone back down on my desk. I still felt angry at Face for being so laid-back on the matters of Chibi and Doctor Six. He seemed to be awfully at ease with Chibi being punished and with the doctor being dismissed from the company. I wished I could argue with Face about his unjust actions against them, but I did not have enough authority to debate with him on the subject. Perhaps I could slowly work my way up the status ladder in the company, and hopefully by that time, I could properly confront Face about the issue.

I heard my office room door open. I turned around and saw Helen enter the room. She wore her usual business suit, and in her right hand was a rolled-up newspaper. She had a weary appearance on her face. "Good morning, Mister Third One," Helen said softly, without smiling. I guessed she was up late last night as well; she probably couldn't sleep well because of the fact that Doctor Six was no longer a part of our company. I wondered if she knew that Chibi was punished this morning due to acting out against the dismissal of Doctor Six.

"Good morning, Helen," I replied back, smiling lightly without baring my teeth. Helen did not smile back; she maintained her tired facial expression. She walked next to my bed and tossed the newspaper onto it. The newspaper rolled open as soon as it landed on the bed, and I saw this headline printed in bold capital letters on the front page.

Helicopter Terrorist Arrested

A headshot photograph of Isaac Warren, the man I formerly knew as Doctor Six, graced the space below the headline. I picked up the newspaper and read through the article printed below the picture:

A man suspected of masterminding yesterday's terrorist attack in the downtown area, which left over fifty pedestrians unconscious, had turned himself in to the local authorities late last night.

The man, whose name is currently withheld by police for security reasons, was involved in a bizarre roadside gas attack on pedestrians which took place just yesterday at approximately 2 pm. An unmarked helicopter hovering over the downtown area had sprayed a form of sleeping gas on a large crowd of people standing near the aftermath of an unrelated road accident. According to various witnesses, many people had attempted to run away from the direction in which the gas was sprayed, but the rate of the spray was fast enough to reach the people running and eventually rendered them unconscious.

According to more eyewitnesses, at the end of the gas attack on the people, the helicopter hovered lower to the ground and picked up two unidentified pedestrians. A person in the helicopter had opened the door and appeared to motion for the two unknown assailants to jump into the helicopter cabin. After the two mysterious pedestrians hopped inside, the helicopter flew away into the sky, leaving behind a huge cloud of green-colored sleeping gas above the downtown district.

The suspect who turned himself in was confirmed by police officials to be the person who opened the door of the helicopter. He will be questioned about the motives of the attacks as well as the whereabouts of his fellow partners in crime. A full investigation is currently under way.

I read through the newspaper article three times in a row before finally setting the paper back down on my bed. I stood still, staring at the floor, thinking. Isaac Warren had actually turned himself in, I thought. He must have realized that he had made a horrible mistake by attacking the innocent pedestrians, even though he initially found them to be guilty of watching the accident aftermath without helping the victims. He must have finally understood that their 'crime' was too subtle to be considered a threat to society, so he allowed himself to be arrested in order to punish himself for his grave mistake. He abided by the company rules despite being fired from the company.

But deep down inside, I did not like the idea of Isaac Warren being behind bars. I was obviously aware that the mistake he made against the pedestrians was a major felony, but I wished there was a way to talk things over with the police so that he could be freed. Of course, that was not at all possible. Modern law is very strict when it comes to acts of unauthorized violence against people, no matter what reason there is for the violent acts.

I lifted my head back up to see Helen. She did not change her unsmiling facial expression. "What should we do about Doctor Si…I mean, Isaac Warren?" I asked, breaking the unnerving silence between us.

"Nothing, Mister Third One," Helen replied dully, "we do nothing about Isaac Warren. He turned himself in to the police, and now the police will deal with him. We cannot intervene."

Defeated by Helen's blunt response, I agreed dejectedly, "Yeah, I guess you're right. I just hope he will keep himself in good condition while in prison." Then I asked her, "So did you come in my office just to show me the newspaper article?"

Helen bit her lower lip, and then said, "No. That was not the only thing. I also wanted to inform you about your next mission. Do not change the casual clothes you are presently wearing. Your upcoming mission requires that you wear something casual, so no need for you to change. Shaffa will be your partner this time, and the next mission will begin in two hours. Be prepared for it."

Helen started walking to the office room door, but then she stopped and faced me again. "Oh, I almost forgot," she said quickly, her left hand open toward me. "Your report, please."

I went to my desk, picked up the green-colored USB storage device containing my second mission report, walked up to Helen and gave it to her. She put it in her pocket, but then she picked out another USB from her other pocket. She handed this other one to me, and I saw that it was the blue-colored USB which I had given her yesterday, the one in which I had saved the file containing my first report.

Without thanking me, she opened the door, stepped outside my office, then stopped and turned around again. "Good luck on your next mission, Mister Third One," she said.

"Thank you, Helen," I replied. And she closed the door without saying anything back to me.

Yet Another Interlude

Once again, my dear reader, I decided to sleep in the shack for a second night. Now I am awake and writing this third and final interlude. The story that I am writing for you is almost finished, although not quite almost finished. You will have to see how everything goes as I continue with my story.

Also, dear reader, please try not to jump to any conclusions regarding Doctor Six or Face or anybody else. As the story progresses, the truths about those people will be uncovered. I hope that you will be patient until then.

I still have plenty of pages left in the book to complete the rest of my story. There are even enough pages here for me to write more than I want to, if I chose to do so. However, as I mentioned before, I have a deadline which limits me from writing as much as I want. Due to this deadline, I must only write what I can in the very short time given to me.

And now, all worries put aside, I will continue writing my story.

Revelation

I was all set to begin my third mission. I waited for Shaffa, my next mission partner, to arrive at my office. While waiting, I picked up a stray magazine from my desk and plopped myself onto my bed, intending to pass time by reading through it.

While on my back, I looked at the cover of the magazine. It was a fairly old issue of a car magazine, and on the front cover was a vivid photograph of a car. It was the same model of the car that I had driven during my normal life when I lived with my family…

My car.

I realized that I had not driven my car for many days on end. I missed driving it around, driving it to pick up my young sister from her friend's house, driving my father to the airport whenever he needed my help to do so for his business trips, driving to the grocery store to buy food items whenever my mother was too ill to go shopping. I missed driving my car.

I should ask Face if I could drive my car sometimes, I thought. I should definitely ask him about that. After all, now that my car has been stored in the company warehouse, it was as much a major part of the company as I was.

I set the magazine aside on the bed and closed my eyes. I decided to rest for a while until Shaffa gets here. Either I wake up on my own, or her entering the room will wake me up.

And sure enough, after about twenty minutes of sleep, I woke up to hear the sound of my door opening and someone entering the room. I looked to the direction of the door and saw Shaffa. She was wearing casual clothes as well; she wore a black shirt with the word 'CLASSIC' printed in green letters at the front, and she also wore a pair of blue jeans and brown sneakers. This is the first time I saw Shaffa wear something other than a uniform.

"Hello, Third One," Shaffa began. "I am here to work with you in the next mission."

I nodded and replied, "Yeah, Helen was here earlier and told me that you would be working with me this time."

Shaffa smiled and said, "Okay, come with me." I got up off of the bed and walked with her to the elevator. Once the elevator door opened, she stepped inside first, and then I followed. The elevator door closed behind us.

As I felt the elevator descending towards the ground floor, I looked at Shaffa's still-smiling face. There was something odd about her smiling most of the time; the smiles were almost robotic. The only instances where I saw her not smiling were when I was confronted on the rooftop by Doctor Six, and also when Face had confronted Doctor Six on that same day. During those parts of the day, Shaffa had a neutral expression on her face, just like Helen's facial expression on those same occasions and this morning. But unlike Helen, whose neutral expression remained the same even until today, Shaffa's smiley face came back and showed no signs of ever being changed before. I somehow found Shaffa to be the oddest member of this company, despite her lack of special attributes currently possessed by the likes of the other company members.

Once the elevator reached the ground floor and opened its doors, Shaffa gestured to me to step out first. I gestured back so that she could go out before me, but then she said, "After you, Third One." I listened to her and walked out of the elevator, with her following behind me. I looked around the lobby and noticed that Helen was not sitting at the reception desk. *Perhaps she was busy today*, I thought.

Shaffa and I exited the company building. Yet again, I saw that the humongous parking lot was practically empty, except for one vehicle parking on the handicap parking space.

And that vehicle was my car!

I smiled involuntarily upon gazing at the car. I felt like it had been ages since I had last seen it in front of me. The car looked just as clean and shiny as it was the last time I saw it in the company warehouse. The company really took good care of its exterior.

Shaffa broke my gaze when she tapped my shoulder. I looked at her and saw that in her open right hand was the car key I had regularly used to drive my car. "For this mission, *you* must drive," Shaffa said to me. I took the key from her, unlocked the car, and opened the driver's side door. The interior of my car was just as clean as its exterior. I was happy that the company had taken great care of my car while I had not driven it for a long time. I sat inside and closed my door. Once Shaffa got inside the passenger's side and closed her door, I started the engine. I heard the familiar roar of my car's engine; it sounded just as fresh as when I drove it long ago. I smiled in satisfaction.

I turned to Shaffa, who was also smiling but for reasons unknown to me, and asked her, "Where is the location of this mission?"

She replied with a question, "Do you remember where the company warehouse is?"

I thought to myself for a second, and then I responded, "Yes, I remember where the warehouse is. Is that where our mission will be?"

Shaffa nodded, still smiling. So I departed from the parking area and drove towards the direction of the company warehouse.

There was a bit of traffic in front of me, so I slowed down to a stop and set the gear to neutral, waiting for the traffic to move. A traffic signal shined a red light was a few cars ahead of us, which explained why the traffic did not move. I tilted my head back on the headrest of my seat and waited quietly and patiently.

Not a word was said between Shaffa and me until about a minute later, when she asked me out of the blue, "Do you have any secrets?"

The strange question he had asked me made me quickly turn my head to her. "What do you mean by that?" I asked harshly, honestly confused about her rather random question.

Suddenly, I heard the loud honking of a truck's horn behind me. I looked in my rearview mirror and saw the truck moving closer to me, and then I looked in front and noticed that the vehicles ahead of me had all sped away because the traffic light color turned green. I hurriedly pressed on the accelerator and my car rocketed past the signal before it turned back to red.

After passing the intersection, I rubbed my eyes with one hand in order to focus my concentration on the road. Once my attention to the road was stable enough, I repeated my question to Shaffa again (but in a nicer yet firm tone this time), "What do you mean by that?"

I glanced at Shaffa and saw that she was still smiling. Her constant smile was really annoying me right now. When will this girl stop smiling unnecessarily?

She replied, "You know, secrets. Things that people hide from each other. Do you have any secrets? Because I have secrets."

What Shaffa was saying was very suspicious. I decided to play along with her. "Tell me your secrets first," I insisted, glancing at her and then looking back to the road. She still smiled, although I noticed she had a sharp look in her eyes, as if she was showing some hostility towards me. I cautiously kept my mind alert just in case she wanted to try anything against me.

"Okay, I will tell you my secrets," Shaffa said. "But not all secrets, only some secrets."

"Fair enough," I said to her casually. "Tell me what you know." Without looking back at Shaffa's ever-smiling face, I kept my eyes on the road and listened as she began talking:

"Evil is very close to me, no matter how good I am. The evil is also very close to our manager, and also Isaac Warren and Helen and Chibi. The evil will soon cause our company to destroy itself."

Her words felt like a joke to me. I felt angered at Shaffa for talking in such a mysterious tone; I wanted to know exactly what she was getting at. I quickly swerved to the side of the road and braked so hard that the tires screeched before the car came to a stop. I looked crossly at Shaffa and shouted at her, "What are you talking about? You're not making any sense!"

Shaffa stayed dead still for some moments, but her face still had that annoying smile. "I am talking about something that you should know, something that no one in the company told you before. Now please, Third One, continue driving and listen to what I must say."

I calmed myself down by breathing slowly in and out, and then I slowly drove back onto the road. "Okay," I said softly, "tell me more." I listened carefully as Shaffa continued her speech:

"Our company is a very good company; we always do many things to help people. However, by helping people we attract evil to ourselves. And this evil becomes even stronger because of another company that looks like ours, but does the exact opposite things we do."

I felt a tingle in my spine after hearing him mention this other company. Was there really a different company similar to the one I that was working for, which specialized in doing evil deeds instead of good deeds? I kept on listening.

"This other company created a chemical that is in the form of a transparent mist and its employees sprayed it inside our main company building in every room. No one can see where it is or what it looks like, except me. I don't know how I am able to see the mist, but I can see it clearly. It is a mist that, when breathed in, generates evil thoughts in people that overtake their good thoughts. It takes a long time to have an effect, but now it is taking effect on everyone in our company."

This was all too new to me; I had to interrupt Shaffa's informative but bizarre speech. "How did you know all this?" I asked hastily.

Shaffa replied, "I know about these things because I was part of that evil company in the past. It was many years ago, their leader told me of the plan to wipe out the good company, the one that I am now working in. He told me that he would send his employees to our main building, but they would be disguised as building inspectors and jobseekers.

"These impostors pretended to look for problems in the building, but they were actually secretly spraying the mist around the building. They open and close their left hands to spray the mist from the pores of their hands. Like this." Shaffa demonstrated her explanation by opening and closing her left hand repetitively. "The people in charge of the security cameras did not find them suspicious because it looked like they were only opening and closing their hands naturally and involuntarily; it looked as natural as a person stretching his or her arms when waking up from sleep. The evil company's undercover employees timed everything so well.

"The fake jobseekers were present to further distract the camera operators in the building. They were given more camera attention because they had no clearance of any kind and were more prone to causing a disturbance. Building inspectors, on the other hand, normally have a certain level of clearance and therefore are expected to behave in an orderly manner without engaging in suspicious activities. So the security camera operators probably neglected thorough monitoring of the fake inspectors and instead focused more on the fake jobseekers instead. In the end, the good company never found out about the evil mist being spread around the building."

I was confused as to how exactly the mist was sprayed from the 'pores of their hands.' That part really made no sense whatsoever to me. "Okay Shaffa," I interrupted again, "just how did these fake inspectors spray the gas directly from their hands?"

Shaffa responded, "That will take me very long to explain, but to put it short and simply, those employees posing as fake inspectors were genetically engineered humans. They can give off the mist from their left hands whenever they needed to do so. Their insides were practically made of the mist after their genetic modifications were completed."

My spine tingled again. So this 'evil' company had the power to genetically modify its own employees so that they could carry out their evil deeds that way? This was all very difficult for me to believe, even after all that I had seen following my employment into the 'good' company. It just did not make any sense. Just how was this mist invisible to everyone except Shaffa, and how can it cause people to think evilly? My only guess was that this 'evil invisible mist' was merely a kind of psychoactive drug that negatively affects the brain. But even with that idea in mind, it didn't make sense how the employees of the evil company were able to emit the mist from their own hands!

"And ever since the evil gas was sprayed in our main company building," Shaffa continued, "everyone in the building was becoming slowly affected by it. The mist particles have stayed embedded inside the building ever since, never showing any signs of dissolving. To make matters worse, the particles can also cling to people and get transmitted from person to person. I myself feel the evil creeping into my heart. No one in the company is safe from this evil, not even the manager. We will all be separated soon, and the company will no longer exist as a result."

Shaffa took a break from her speech. I glimpsed at her for a moment and saw that she finally lost her smile. "You don't have to believe what I just told you, Third One, but please keep everything in mind. I know it all sounds strange, but I am telling the truth. I used to be a part of that evil company, but I got fired for saving the life of a civilian. I don't remember why I had joined that evil company in the first place, but I now regret having joined it before. From the day I was fired, I vowed to be good and eventually I was hired by Face for that very reason. I am happy for being a part of this good company, but I fear that the company will soon be gone. I wish I told Face about all this from the beginning, but now it's too late because he won't believe anything that I just told you. The evil has already got to him."

She took a deep breath. Then she said, "This evil mist is not only limited to the main company building. The leader of the evil company also planned to spread the mist to the rest of the world. The mist will make many evil things happen, such as more fighting, ignorance, and even the breaking up of families."

The breaking up of families.

Right after Shaffa mentioned it, I remembered that before I joined the 'good' company, my father acted very strange when he pushed me against the wall, when he was furious about my not having a job at that time. I remembered his angry face, his eyes all red and blood-shot. I also remembered how my friend Mark overreacted in an unusually angry manner by fiercely tossing his controller onto the floor, right after I had simply told him to stop playing games and find a job.

Perhaps they were both affected by the mist somehow. At this point, after all the strange incidents that happened subsequent to my graduating from university, and after listening to Shaffa's speech full of revealed secrets, I was positively convinced that the mist was the main reason for their sudden anger towards me. I also believed that the mist had indeed affected Doctor Six and Face, and may soon affect the others, including myself, if no action was taken to stop the mist and its effects on people.

Nevertheless, I decided it was best to concentrate on my current mission. I silently promised myself in my mind that I would attempt to confront Face about this problem.

I finally said to Shaffa, "You know, for the most part I am starting to believe what you told me. How about if we both discuss the issue of the mist with Face once we complete this mission? That way, maybe Face will believe you. Two heads are better than one, after all."

I looked at Shaffa and saw that her robot smile had returned, a little brighter than before. "I like your confident attitude towards this issue," Shaffa said vibrantly. "Yes, let's do that after we complete the mission. With your help, Face should finally believe me and take action against the menace of the evil mist."

With that, I drove faster through the streets in order to quickly get to the company warehouse to begin the next mission.

Execution

Once we finally reached the warehouse, I stopped the car in front of the entrance and honked the horn three times so that someone inside would open the gate for us. Eventually, after exactly one second, the gate opened. I drove slowly into the warehouse, and after parking in the middle of the huge main room I stepped out of the car, and Shaffa also got out. Turning my head slowly while standing in my spot, I looked around the warehouse.

As I had seen before, the main room of the warehouse was lit up by the lights hanging from the ceiling. The vehicles I saw in the warehouse before were still there: The white limousine, the mammoth military-like pickup truck, the tow truck, Helen's ambulance, and the four black-colored luxury cars. They were all parked at the far end of the warehouse, in the same positions as they were from the last time I had seen them. I noticed the empty space between the limousine and the pickup truck, where I had previously seen my own car parked the last time I was here. The warehouse crates were still here as well, although some of them have been noticeably opened up and tipped over, their contents emptied on the floor: small cardboard boxes and wooden furniture items lay scattered near the opened crates.

I looked to my right and saw a boxy-shaped gas furnace next to the right wall of the warehouse. Its lid was open, exposing orange flames of fire. Grey smoke rose from the fires in the furnace towards the ceiling, suspiciously not activating the emergency water sprinklers attached above. Either the warehouse smoke detectors were faulty today, or they were deactivated. What was an open furnace doing in a place like this, where there were many flammable materials surrounding it?

"Third One," Shaffa broke my trail of thoughts, "we must find water to pour on the fire in that furnace. This is our mission."

I stared at her, confused. What was the point of pouring water on the fire, when the most logical way to stop the fire in this situation was to simply switch off the furnace? As long as the furnace was still activated and steadily feeding with fire, dousing the flames with water was pointless. Better to simply turn this contraption off to cut the flow, I thought.

"But couldn't we just turn the gas off?" I asked her, prepared to argue if she insisted on uselessly using water to put the fire out.

"The gas flowing to the furnace cannot be stopped," Shaffa said. "Face told me that there was a problem with the switch, so the gas pipe system will continuously feed the fire. Also, all the fire extinguishers in the warehouse have gone missing; nobody knows what happened or who took them. The only thing we can do is pour water on the flames so that the fire doesn't accidentally spread to anything in here. However, Face said that he will send in reinforcements to fix the switch so that the furnace can be turned off."

Even after she gave me a valid reason for using water to extinguish the furnace fire, bothersome questions in my mind challenged her reasoning: What kind of mission was this? How was this mission related to helping good people or stopping evildoers? Why was Shaffa taking this suspiciously awkward mission seriously?

I pushed the niggling questions aside and decided to just follow orders and complete this mission quickly. It seemed to be a ridiculously easy mission, and I wanted to quickly finish it so that Shaffa and I could go talk to Face.

"Alright, let's do this," I exclaimed. I walked around, looking carefully for anything that looked like a water container. Some seconds later, I saw a red bucket filled with water sitting next to the warehouse office door. I picked up the bucket with both hands and ran to the furnace, carefully avoiding spilling the water. I swung the bucket to the direction of the furnace, and the water splashed all over the inside of the furnace, hitting the fiery flames with a strong hissing sound. Most of the fire had disappeared into a gray-white smoky vapor, but the flames were slowly coming back as a result of the defective gas system continually bringing the fire back to life in the furnace.

I turned back to see where Shaffa had gone. She had disappeared; she was probably hunting for more water containers in the labyrinth of crates stacked around in the warehouse. At first, I was going to call out to her to ask if she found any water, but instead I decided to patiently wait for her to come back. The flames would not get big fast enough to spread out of the furnace just yet, I thought to myself.

All of a sudden, I heard a door open. I turned around and saw that somebody had opened the warehouse office door, the door that had the word 'office' written on it. I saw Face step outside the office, wearing his trench coat and fedora, with two men whom were unfamiliar to me. The man walking right behind Face had a light mustache and beard, and a very pale complexion which even rivaled that of Face. The other man with him had no facial hair at all and had a more tanned skin tone, and was considerably fatter than the thin pale-skinned bearded man behind Face.

A fat man and a thin man.

I suddenly remembered Helen's story, about the mysterious fat man and thin man whom burned down Chibi's house, while she and Helen were still inside. Were these two men the same ones who almost killed Chibi and Helen? I shuddered at the thought. But then, I silently told myself in my mind that it would be too much of a coincidence if these two men accompanying Face were the same arsonists from Helen's past.

Putting my thoughts on hold, I focused on the two men. The thin man was carrying a toolbox in his left hand. The fat man was clasping a miniature table with both hands, and there was something attached to the top of the table. I waited for the three men to come closer so that I could get a better look.

"Hey there, Third One!" Face greeted enthusiastically. "Well done on putting out the first fire. Your job here is done." He snapped his fingers and said, "Keith, please fix the switch of the furnace and then turn it all off. It's getting too hot in here."

I saw the thin man run towards the furnace. Face had ordered the thin man named Keith as if he was one of his associates. Perhaps Keith and the other man were company employees that I had not met yet, I thought. Face will most probably introduce me to the two men formally as soon as Keith repairs the gas system and turns off the furnace.

"Congratulations, Third One," Face said to me, "you have completed your third mission." Then he laughed loudly, the same laugh I had heard from him when I met him the every first time. Then he stopped laughing and said, "I just realized that this mission was your third mission, and you are nicknamed 'The Third One.' That's just too funny!"

I allowed a fake smile to form on my face and then forced myself to laugh at Face's unfunny joke. Face gave me a weird look, as if he knew full well that I did not find his joke to be funny at all. I heard clanking sounds behind me; Keith was busy repairing the gas system of the furnace with the tools he had with him. Each clanking sound from Keith's tools coming in contact with the metallic pipes seemed to chisel away the strange look on Face.

"Alright, Third One," Face began, "we need to talk about a few things regarding your fellow colleague Chibi. You see, Chibi has not been behaving well ever since I fired Doctor Six from the company, so I felt that she needs more discipline. I want you to stand here with me, and watch how Keith and Greg punish her. Greg? Please place the table on the floor."

I saw the fat man, named Greg, slowly set the table on the floor as per the orders given by Face. Then I saw exactly what was attached to the top of the table.

It was Chibi.

Her arms and legs were strapped down by strips of dark purple tape, with each strip holding her limbs to the surface of the small table. Her eyes looked as blank as usual, but her plushy cotton face looked very moist, as if she was crying earlier. She did not move at all.

A surge of anger filled my brain and my heart. I started to run to Chibi to set her free, but then the fat man named Greg quickly grabbed me and took me back to where Face was standing.

"Let go of me!" I shouted. I squirmed with all my might but I could not get free from Greg's tough grip. He twisted my arms behind my back. I cringed; this scenario reminded me of that time in my first mission with Doctor Six and Chibi, when the bulky tanned gang member tightly held both my hands behind my back to prevent me from doing anything.

"Now now, Third One, calm down," Face said in a gentle tone of voice. "I don't want to have to punish you too." I looked at him with fury in my eyes, but then I purposely took a deep breath to calm myself down. "That's good, Third One. Greg, please let him go."

Greg let go of my arms and lightly nudged me closer to Face. Then he knelt down to the small table that Chibi was tied on. I felt deeply angry inside, but I made a decision to keep myself calm. It was no good trying to save Chibi right now, especially when I was up against Greg and my own manager. Even Keith would most probably provide Greg and Face with support to restrain me if I caused any commotion against them. Alone, I was overpowered and helpless against the three men.

Then I remembered Shaffa. Where was she anyway? Was she staying hidden because I had almost caused a ruckus for the first time in front of Face and his associates? Or was she afraid of watching Chibi be punished mercilessly? I hoped she would show up soon, because I needed someone to help me in case Face decided to punish me next for whatever reason.

"Now that everyone is calm," Face began, "allow me to explain how Chibi will be disciplined today." I saw Keith walk over to us with his toolbox in hand, and then he knelt down next to the table on which Chibi was tied. He opened the toolbox and picked out a…

Scalpel.

My stomach felt like it was being joined into a knot. I seriously wanted to lunge at Keith, take away that scalpel from him, and throw it into the furnace to burn it away. But of course, doing so would be dangerous and stupid, as I could accidentally cut myself with the scalpel while taking it away from Keith. And even if I managed to take it away from him without a scratch, throwing the scalpel into the furnace would be futile at this point since Keith fixed the fault in the furnace gas system and switched off the entire mechanism. And besides, I was outnumbered three to one because Shaffa was hiding somewhere in the maze of crates. I had to keep myself calm so that nothing bad would happen.

"During the last time Chibi was punished," Face explained, "she was given a beating using plastic sticks. But even after her light punishment, she was stubbornly not following my simple orders. So now, she will receive an even greater punishment. My associate Keith here will use that scalpel to cut off her right arm so that she can think more about the mistakes she made. And if she makes any more mistakes, harsher disciplinary measures will follow. I want you, Third One, to witness this punishment so that you never think about making the same mistakes as Chibi did."

Face took a small hand-sized box out of his pocket. He opened the lid of the box, let the contents slide out into his hand, and then tossed the box to the floor. He had a deck of playing cards in his hands, which he was briskly shuffling. "There are only thirty-three cards in this deck, as opposed to fifty-two cards and two joker cards," Face said. "Do you know why there are only thirty three cards, Third One?"

I shook my head and responded, "No, I don't know why. Tell me."

Face stopped shuffling the cards and explained, "I had used these cards to keep track of how many times she talked during her punishment last night. Each card represents one word, so each time she said one word to me, I threw away one card. You see, before punishing her, I told her to keep quiet and not say a word. And I told her that if she uttered one word during the punishment, insulting or otherwise, then I would get rid of one card. I told her that I would keep up this process until no cards were available anymore. And once all the cards are gone, she wouldn't ever be a part of this company again.

"But that's not all. In addition to being fired from the company, I am required to dispose of her. I realized that we cannot have a living doll running around in the real world revealing to everyone where she came from. I know full well that Chibi would tell others about the company if I simply let her go. Therefore, if she runs out of cards, she will ultimately be exterminated from the world itself."

Everything that Face had said made me think of him as an evil mastermind. At this point, it was difficult for me to believe that he was once a good person who was friendly and caring towards his employees. Now he was behaving in exactly the opposite manner from before, so much so that he seemed to have transformed into a completely different person. But based on what Shaffa had told me, the reason why he had changed so much was because of this 'evil' mist that an evil company had created and spread everywhere in our main company building. I hoped that this mist would not affect me any time soon, because if I succumb to the effects of the mist, then Chibi's life would be at stake.

"And by the way, Third One," Face continued, "should Chibi's cards run out, *you* will be the one to eliminate Chibi. If you do that, your salary will be tripled and I will personally make sure that you get to see your family again. And if you choose not to eradicate her, then I will fire you right here on the spot and turn you in to the authorities. The choice is yours."

So far, everything that Face had said to me since his appearance in the warehouse today was pure evil. The effects of the mist had definitely spread through him like wildfire through a forest. I wished I could do something about it, but at the moment, I could not do anything against the evil that coursed within him. I had to keep myself cool in order to slowly and carefully solve the problem.

"Okay," I responded after a deep breath, "I will be responsible for Chibi's execution if all her chance cards run out."

I actually had no intention whatsoever of getting rid of Chibi; I only said that to satisfy Face so that he doesn't lash out at me in anger. It was true that I wanted to see my parents and my young sister again, but sacrificing the life of an innocent person for the sake of meeting my family was not the right way. My priority was to save Chibi from impending doom, and only after that would I think of what to do about Face. Right now, my family was the last thing on my mind.

"No Omar! Please don't kill me!"

I heard the familiar-sounding tiny little girl voice scream those words from the small table. Greg, upon hearing Chibi scream unexpectedly, jumped up and almost fell over backwards. Keith also jumped slightly, although not as much as the elephant-sized Greg. Face scowled and immediately flung in the air several playing cards from the deck he was holding. The cards fell gracelessly to the ground, with each card landing far apart from the other.

"Twenty-seven cards left, Chibi," Face remarked harshly. Then his scowl melted into a smile when he said, "Keith, please begin the operation – I mean, the punishment. And Greg, be on the ready in case anything gets out of hand."

Both Keith and Greg nodded. Greg kneeled down again next to the small table where Chibi was strapped down. Keith also kneeled down, carefully holding the scalpel in his hand. I noticed that Chibi was struggling to break free from the purple tape that kept her stuck on the table. I saw miniature teardrops forming below her eyes, and her mouth was in the shape of a sad pout. Despite being stuck to the table, her wriggling around was so powerful that the table looked like it was vibrating while she struggled.

But how come she could not break away from the purple tape? Was that tape really strong enough to keep her down?

My thoughts were broken by Keith when he shouted, "Stop moving around! Boss, tell her to stop moving, I can't properly cut her arm this way."

Face then said to Chibi, "Chibi, please stop moving around and let Keith do his job properly. You can never break free from the tape; it's a special tape that Doctor Six created when he was with us. It's strong enough to resist people and things that possess special abilities, meaning you can't break free from the tape yourself. So settle down, little brat; you cannot escape your punishment."

Chibi stopped struggling and turned her head to look at him. Then she screamed again in her high-pitched voice, "I won't listen to you! You're a monster! You fired Doctor Six and now you're using his things that he made! You're a monster!"

Face cringed while Chibi screamed at him. Then after Chibi finished, Face took more cards from the deck and tossed them in the air. They all landed in random places on the warehouse floor. "You only have six cards left, Chibi," Face told her. He fanned out the cards in his left hand and declared, "After these are gone, you will be executed."

Chibi suddenly jerked the table so hard that the table jumped almost three feet in the air, and then landed down to the floor with a small thump. Greg jumped away again, and Keith cried out in pain as he accidentally cut himself on his left arm with the scalpel. I saw blood trickle out of the wound and onto the ground in drops. He threw the scalpel to the floor and clutched the wound with his right hand in an attempt to stop the leakage. Greg fumbled in his pocket, pulled out wads of tissue paper, and handed them to Keith. Keith took the tissues and held them over the wound to soak up the blood.

Chibi screamed again at Face, "Third One would never kill me! He's my *friend*! But you're *not* my friend anymore, Face! You're a *monster*!"

Face violently threw the final six cards in the air, and once again, they all landed onto the floor in randomized positions. He looked really angry now; he frowned and his eyes were reddened and blood-shot, exactly like my father's eyes when he acted furiously due to the effects of the mysterious mist.

Face stomped over to Chibi, stood over her, and said to her, "Well, Chibi, it looks like your cards literally ran out. You may have saved yourself from losing your arm, but you can't save yourself from your ultimate punishment."

He walked back to me and gently shoved me towards the table. "Third One, please pick up the scalpel," Face ordered, pointed at the scalpel that lay on the floor. I took a few steps and cautiously picked up the scalpel. Its blade was now stained with Keith's blood. Greg handed me a tissue paper, and I took it from him to clean the blade. Then I let go of the blood-stained tissue paper and watched it fall to the floor.

"Keith and Greg," Face addressed, "please come here and stand with me. Third One, step closer to the table and stay there facing Chibi. After the end of my speech of honor, you may perform Chibi's execution."

I moved closer to the table and faced Chibi. A mixture of sadness and anger was displayed on her face. I stared at her solemnly. I could hear her faintly quiet sobs as Face began his speech:

"In the honor of this glorious company of ours, I hereby dismiss Chibi from the company forever due to extreme misconduct. She may never return to the company ever again, nor will she go and stay with anyone. In addition, she will be removed from this world due to her possessing inhuman powers that would never be deemed acceptable by human society. She will be honorably executed for the good of herself, the company, and the world. Once eliminated, a replacement will be in order to fill in her position.

"Third One, please stab Chibi in her heart to end her life. By doing so, you will be promoted to one of the top positions in the company, and as promised to you earlier I will personally see to it that you meet your family again. Please begin the execution now, Third One."

I gulped down my saliva and knelt down beside Chibi. Her face was so moist with tears, and she breathed in quick bursts, her chest rapidly heaving up and down. She turned her face away from me and lay as still as she could. I lifted the scalpel above her chest, closing my eyes tightly.

Agony

Time seemed to slow down to the pace of a tortoise losing a race to a hare. I felt like I was holding the scalpel over Chibi's chest for hours on end when, in reality, I only held it above her for a few seconds. I was deeply in thought, thinking of what I was going to do next.

"Go on, Third One," Face urged softly, "don't fail me now. I promise to promote you right after you do the job of executing Chibi. And don't forget that I will also allow you to meet your family again. Now finish the job, Third One. I don't have all day."

I hesitated. I lifted the scalpel even higher above Chibi's chest, and then I let my hand slowly descend. Chibi continued keeping her gaze away from me, probably fearing the sight of the scalpel blade and the helpless expression on my face. Now the blade was an inch away from her chest. I was going to move the scalpel further, but then…

Then I pulled the scalpel away from the direction of her chest, and gently set it down on the floor.

"Don't worry, Chibi," I said assuredly, "I won't hurt you."

Chibi turned her head towards me, and I saw a light smile form on her face. She stared at me with her doll eyes, silently thanking me for sparing her life.

I stood up and boldly turned around to the direction of Face and his goons. Face looked extremely angry, and Keith and Greg both had their eyebrows raised in disbelief. Greg was going to walk towards me, but Face put his left hand up to stop him. "I'll deal with him," Face insisted. Greg took a step back to where he was initially standing. Face then walked over to me and kneed me very hard in the stomach. I instantly fell to the floor, coughing and gagging like Doctor Six when Face had punched him in the stomach.

"You are the biggest fool, Third One," Face said firmly. I looked up from the ground and saw that he still had that angry expression on his face. "You are a disgrace to the original employee before you that was nicknamed 'The Third One.' How dare you disobey my order? Don't you want to see your family again?"

I stopped coughing and responded to him warily, while still lying on the ground, "I would never want to kill a friend just to see my family again. Chibi is my friend, and so are Shaffa, Helen, and Doctor Six." I coughed some more, then continued, "You were once a friend, too, Face...but now you've changed. You're evil now, and you don't realize it. If I had killed Chibi, then meeting my family again wouldn't matter to me anymore. I wouldn't want to see my family ever again if it means I have to hurt or kill a friend."

Face started laughing, his laugh echoing throughout the warehouse. He then kicked me hard in the side of my stomach. I groaned involuntarily after the impact, and looked up angrily at him. He smiled evilly at me and said, "Alright, Third One, if that's how you feel." He crossed his arms and declared, "You're *fired*. As of today, you are no longer a part of the company, and you will no longer be known as 'The Third

One.' Henceforth, you will be known by your real name 'Omar.' And since you are not part of the company anymore, you will be turned in to the authorities for your blatantly dangerous misbehavior in the company."

I felt hands pick me up from the ground. Keith and Greg had pulled me to my feet and put my hands behind my back, restraining me. Face walked towards the warehouse office room and stood next to the door. Then he said, "I will find someone to replace you very soon, Omar. Keith and Greg will escort you to the nearest police station and explain everything to them so that they can officially arrest you. But before they do that, I would like you to meet the newest member of the company."

Face opened the office door and left it open. A person then emerged from the office. I recognized this person. It was Jassim, the leader of the neighborhood gang from when I had undergone my first mission with Doctor Six and Chibi. He was wearing a black business suit and sported the same pink trilby on his head that I had seen him wear in the mansion. Was he not apprehended by the police like his fellow gang members?

Jassim saw me and smiled. Face put his left hand on Jassim's shoulder and said, "I'm sure you remember this man, Omar. His name is Jassim, and he was the leader of the gang that you, Doctor Six, and Chibi were up against."

"Yeah, I know," I replied. "Isn't he supposed to be behind bars along with his gang?"

Face then responded, "Actually, Jassim here managed to escape from the mansion before the police arrived, so he avoided being arrested unlike his cronies. Once I heard that the police had failed to apprehend Jassim, I decided to send

Keith and Greg out to search for him. Within a day, they found him hiding out at an abandoned junkyard just outside of town. They brought him over to me, and when I told Jassim that I would give him to the police, he broke down in tears, confessed his crimes, and vowed never to live a life of crime again. I was so moved by his confession that I decided to recruit him into the company. I also recruited Keith and Greg in a similar fashion."

I narrowed my eyes, flabbergasted at what Face was saying. I exclaimed, "So criminals that cry for mercy after their crimes are accepted directly into the company just like that? That is so narrow-minded!"

Face, seemingly ignoring my words, simply said, "Long story short, I saw some good in these three men, and so far, they were successful in perfectly obeying my orders, unlike you, Doctor Six, and Chibi."

Face walked ahead of Jassim, pointed at the table with his left hand, and said, "Okay Jassim, you remember the talking doll I was telling you about the other day? The one named Chibi? That's her on that little table. I want you to pick up the scalpel and execute her by stabbing her in the heart."

Jassim looked at the scalpel that lay on the floor, and then he laughed derisively and said, "That is too small! I will use my knife." He reached into his left pocket and pulled out a switchblade.

"Very well," Face said. "Now go to the little doll and execute her. Do not be afraid of her powers; she is tied down securely and cannot use her powers against you."

Jassim nodded his head, his smile widening. I assumed that Face had already exposed the information about supernatural elements of the company to Jassim when he recruited him, which would explain why Jassim was not at all surprised when Face mentioned a 'talking doll' with 'powers.' I also assumed that the evil mist had spread to Jassim as well, since he readily followed Face's evil order to execute Chibi without any hesitation whatsoever. He walked to the table, knelt down, and readied the switchblade above Chibi's chest.

"Now that there are no more interruptions, we can finally begin with the execution of Chibi," Face stated. "Jassim, please begin. And Chibi, may your soul rest in peace."

I lowered my gaze to the floor and closed my eyes tightly, silently praying for a miracle to save Chibi while holding back the tears accumulating behind my eyelids.

Interruption

A car engine started. I quickly lifted my head up and opened my eyes, and saw that Jassim did not perform Chibi's execution. In fact, Jassim was now away from the table, eyes fearfully widened, holding his knife with both hands and looking to the area of the warehouse where the vehicles were parked. Face, Keith, and Greg also looked to that direction. The execution was interrupted just in the nick of time.

The pickup truck with camouflage markings barreled down towards us, its engine roaring like a mad lion. Jassim rushed inside the warehouse office room, and Keith and Greg followed him. Face ignored his three cowardly henchmen and continued staring at the approaching truck. I dashed to the little table that Chibi was on, picked up the table with both hands (it was surprising lighter than it appeared), and ran away from the direction of the oncoming truck. The truck came closer and closer to Face, until it screeched to a complete stop just three feet in front of him. Face continued staring at the truck, unfazed.

I saw that the driver of the pickup truck was none other than Shaffa. She stepped out of the truck and walked up to Face. "Hello there, Face," Shaffa greeted with a smile.

Face grabbed Shaffa by her shirt, pulled her close, and spoke fiercely, "Shaffa, just what on earth do you think you are doing? You were supposed to depart from this place and leave Third behind after the mission was completed. You will be punished for disobeying my orders, as well as for interrupting a major employee dismissal ceremony, and for nearly running me over with a company vehicle."

Then, with surprising strength, Shaffa forcibly pushed Face away, breaking free from Face's grasp. Face nearly toppled over backwards as a result of Shaffa's sudden strong push. "You haven't been behaving like yourself lately, Face, Shaffa said sternly. "Your mind has been corrupted by evil, and as a result, you are not aware anymore that what you are doing is full of wickedness. I told you before, there is an evil company conspiring to end the life of our own company. They sprayed a chemical mist in many places in the city, including our very own main building, and it's affecting you and everyone else. If we don't stop this mist from spreading further, then this company will cease to exist in a matter of days. And without the existence of this good company, the safety of the world will be at stake."

Face gave Shaffa a questioning look. "Shaffa..." he started, but then his voice trailed off, unable to speak. His face looked flushed as if from exhaustion.

Shaff smiled widely, her eyes seemingly staring through Face as she continued, "In truth, I used to be one of the employees of that evil company, but I got fired for doing a good deed. After I lost my job there, I decided to do good deeds for people and never return to my old ways again. I did things like tutoring children of poorer families that could not afford to send their kids to proper schools, and helping clean up the litter around the city in all weather conditions.

"Then of course, thanks to your company's high-tech employment services, you found out about me and my good ways, and then you hired me. I am very happy to be an employee of your company, Face. But I deeply regret lying to you before about my background and my real self; the lie itself was an evil deed of mine that may have given the mist a stronger effect on you. I did not try hard enough to convince you about the effects of the mist.

"My fears kept me from properly telling you the truth sooner, but I am not afraid anymore. During me and Third One's drive to the warehouse, I already told him about everything I had just told you. With his help, I will try to remove the effects of the mist from you to prevent you from destroying our company."

After Shaffa's speech was done, Face laughed ever so loudly. He laughed so hard that he held his sides with his hands. After he stopped laughing, he caught his breath and said, "Shaffa…you're one crazy robot."

My eyes twitched. "Robot…Shaffa is a robot?" I murmured.

Shaffa still kept her smile displayed. I always felt that her mannerisms were very mechanical, but I never would have guessed that she was an actual robot.

"You obviously don't remember your background, Shaffa," Face continued, now grinning almost like Shaffa as if mimicking her smile. "You are a Humanoid Experimental Robot; or HER for short. That other company created dozens of HERs like you to carry out their operations and programmed you all to be evil, but somehow your operating system defied their programming matrix, and they had no idea how to make your system operate like the other HERs. They didn't fire you; I had sent my own covert operatives to break you out and then I had you internally reprogrammed to *think* you were fired."

I stood motionless, still holding the table that Chibi was tied to. Chibi was also silent, looking and listening to Face.

"After your reprogramming, I let my associates take you to a deserted part of town and leave you there, to see what you would do if you were alone. As I expected, you made your way back to the city and started doing good deeds. When I saw you do all that, I hired you."

Face stayed quiet after his speech, looking glumly down at the ground. Shaffa kept her expression the same as earlier, and I frowned. This was all difficult for me to fathom!

Suddenly, Face broke the silence. "I still don't believe this mist really exists, and even if it did, I would be the *last* person in the world to be affected by it. For goodness sake Shaffa, I am the *manager* of this company! Everything that I plan out is for the good of human society; there is no way that I would become corrupted by evil. If anything, everyone underneath my position in the company is more prone to corruption than I am."

Shaffa was going to respond to Face's blind speech, but Face raised his hand before Shaffa could speak and told her, "Say no more, Shaffa." Then Face turned around and called out at the top of his lungs, "Keith! Greg! Jassim! Come out here *now*!"

The warehouse office door opened and I saw the three men obediently rush outside. "Keith and Greg, please restrain

Shaffa," Face ordered. "And Jassim, please bring Chibi to me. *I* will be the one to perform Chibi's execution."

Keith and Greg walked up to Shaffa and held her still, even though Shaffa showed no signs of resistance. Jassim walked toward me, switchblade in hand. I defensively held the small table close to my chest with both hands, with Chibi facing me.

I had an idea on how to outsmart Jassim.

I let him come a few inches closer to me. "Give me the table," Jassim said to me harshly. Once he laid his hand on the table, I let the table fall to the floor. Jassim looked at me angrily and was going to say something, but I interrupted him by swiftly hitting his girly pink trilby off his head with my right hand. Surprised, he looked up and saw it fly off of his head and fall on the ground behind him. This distracted him, so I made my move. I quickly took some steps backwards as if to run away, and then I ran as fast as I could towards him. With all my force, I speared him in the stomach with my shoulder, and he fell to the ground. I got up and dusted myself off, looking at his face. His eyes were closed, and he had a neutral sleeping expression on his face. Surprisingly, my tackle had knocked him out cold.

"Third One!" I heard Shaffa cry out. I looked at her and noticed that she was now struggling to break free from the grasps of Keith and Greg. "The tape holding Chibi down only resists supernatural powers! You don't have any special powers, so just pull the tape off and—"

Shaffa's cries were cut short when Greg punched her hard in the stomach. After the blow, Keith and Greg let go of Shaffa and she fell to the ground, coughing chokingly. Now she seemed more human than robot; I guessed this was a result of the faulty programming of her operating system. Perhaps she was programmed to lean more on human thoughts and feelings, even though this was not the intention when she was created.

I listened to Shaffa's instructions and quickly trotted back to where I had dropped the little table. Thankfully, when I had dropped it onto the floor, it had landed on its legs face-up, so Chibi was not hurt when it landed on the solid warehouse ground.

I heard Face shout, "Shut your big mouth, Shaffa!" His shout was followed by thudding sounds. I glanced back and saw that Face was repeatedly pummeling Shaffa with his left foot, kicking her again and again, while Keith and Greg restrained her. At this point, Face's actions really angered me; I seriously wanted to beat him up. However, I decided for the time being to ignore what was happening to Shaffa and concentrated on setting Chibi loose. *I will need Chibi's help to defeat Face and his goons,* I thought.

I crouched down and quickly but with great care started pulling the tapes off of Chibi. First her right arm, then her left. Then her right leg, then her left. She was now free from the strips of tape that held her down.

"Yay! I can move again!" Chibi yelled gleefully. Testing her legs, she walked a few steps away from me, and then back. I was going to pick her up to keep her safe, but then I saw a booted foot suddenly kick her away, sending her light body flying into the air. I looked up and saw that it was Face who had kicked her. He glared at me with a furious expression on his face.

With both hands, Face pulled me up to my feet and grabbed me by my shirt. "I will not accept any of this insolence, Omar," Face said threateningly, his spittle landing on my face. "I will make sure the authorities sentence you to – *aaah*!"

Face shrieked in pain and let go of my shirt. I took some steps back and saw that Chibi was biting Face's left leg. Her mouth, which was normally a curved line on her face, was now opened up, and two sets of teeth stabbed Face's leg. Her teeth looked like the blades of miniature knives. Blood oozed rapidly from Face's leg, so much so that a small puddle of blood had formed next to his injured foot in less than three seconds.

Face screamed in horror and frantically wiggled his injured leg to throw Chibi off, but Chibi's grip on his leg was too strong. Face continued the process until he tripped and fell down, crying out in pain when he landed in a large pool of blood, his own blood. His trench coat was covered in blood, as was his fedora, which had fallen off of his head and into the red puddle. Face groaned for some time but then fell silent, breathing slowly.

Chibi stopped biting Face's leg and lifted her bladed mouth away from it. She walked up to me, her red flower dress soiled in Face's blood. She flashed me a toothy grin, her bladed teeth stained with blood. "Looks like I have to brush my teeth real good tonight!" Chibi declared. Then I saw her knife-like teeth slowly descend back into her plushy cotton face. The razor-sharp teeth were all gone in a matter of seconds, and Chibi's mouth returned back to its original happy-faced curved line form. Chibi would be perfect as a haunted living doll in a horror film, I thought.

I looked around the area and noticed that Shaffa was back on her feet, looking to my direction. I also noticed that Keith and Greg were gone; I assumed that they ran away from the scene after seeing what Chibi had done to their manager. How cowardly of them!

"Did Keith and Greg run back into the office?" I asked Shaffa.

She chuckled happily and said, "They ran outside through the back door of the warehouse. But they won't get far. While I was hiding behind the crates earlier, I called in company reinforcements to guard the area surrounding the warehouse. They will quickly track them down and take them to the police." She then smiled extra wide and said, "I love the perks of being authorized to call for backup."

I smiled. I felt a squeezing sensation on my right ankle. I looked down and saw Chibi hugging my ankle. She said, in her high-pitched voice, "Thank you so much, Third One! You saved my life!"

I suddenly noticed that she had called me 'Third One,' even though Face dismissed me from the company earlier and declared that my real name be used when addressing me. "But Chibi, my name isn't 'Third One' anymore," I told her. "Face fired me, so now my name is Omar again."

Chibi squeezed my leg even harder and insisted, "I don't care what Face said, I will always call you 'Third One!' You deserve that name!"

"She's right," Shaffa agreed. Now Chibi let go of my leg and ran to Shaffa. She started hugging her right leg.

"Oh sorry, Shaffa! I almost forgot about you," she declared. "Thank you for saving my life, too!"

"It's all right, Chibi," Shaffa said, looking at her and smiling. Chibi then stopped hugging her leg and stood next to her. Then the both of them walked over to me. "As I was saying," Shaffa continued, "Chibi is right about you deserving to be named 'The Third One.' You were the only employee in the whole of this company who wasn't affected by the mist in any way. While working for the evil company in the past, I was told that only people who have large amounts of pure goodness in their hearts cannot be affected by the mist. You have a lot of good in you, much more than me and Chibi and everyone else in the company thus far. If I was the manager of this company, I would have let you take my place and let you be in charge of the company."

What Shaffa said to me really made me feel good inside. She was right; I was never affected by this 'mist.' I was always a good person, ever since I was a little boy. In school, I never did the bad things that my peers did. In university, I never took part in activities that caused harm of any kind to others. I was always honest towards people, in my educational and non-educational life, whether I knew them personally or not. I always believed in doing good things for myself and for others, while vigilantly avoiding the bad things in life as much as I was able to.

"Can somebody help me already?" Face shouted, interrupting my thoughts. I looked at him. He lay their helplessly, breathing repetitively, in the pool of his own blood, unable to walk due to his aching leg that still bled continuously like a leaking water faucet.

"Let's get Face to a hospital," Shaffa suggested. "Now that he can't move on his own, this is the perfect time to start removing the effects of the mist contained inside his lungs and brain. But first, his leg injury must be treated."

She walked to the back of the pseudo-military pickup truck, opened the tailgate, and climbed in the back. She put on some gloves, and then picked up what looked like a spare petrol container. "Besides pure goodness," Shaffa started, "another weakness of the mist is smoke from a big fire. In order to rid indoor areas from the effects of the mist, smoke must be present to mix with the chemical properties of the mist particles, and then the smoke eventually overrides the particles and consumes them. Then the mist particles remain inside the 'belly' of the smoke, and once the smoke disappears, so does the mist."

Shaffa set the petrol container down next to me, walked towards the furnace, and turned it on. The flames returned brighter and fierier than before. "The best way to fully rid an indoor place of the mist is to burn the entire place. I will use the liquid gas in that container to make a trail from the furnace to the flammable goods in this warehouse. That way, there will be a fire big enough to engulf this whole place in flames and making enough smoke to eat up all of the mist particles here. And we need not worry about the goods in this warehouse. Lucky for us, only useless spare junk is stored here for recycling purposes, while all the important things such as personal items are stored in other warehouses."

"What about taking Face to the hospital?" I asked.

"Don't worry about our manager, he will be fine," Shaffa assured me. "I will take him – and Jassim there on the floor – to the hospital as soon as I am done with pouring the trail of petrol from the fires to the crates. Take Chibi with you in your car, go back to company headquarters, and inform Helen about the current situation. I'll use the ambulance to drive Face and Jassim to the hospital, so don't worry about a thing. And once you explain the situation to Helen, tell her not to take any action until I get there."

I nodded my head in unison. Shaffa picked up the petrol container and started walking to the furnace to make the gas trail. I picked up Chibi from the ground and ran to my car. I set Chibi down on the passenger seat and started the engine. I was going to reverse out of the warehouse, but then I realized that the electronic main gate was closed. I lowered my window and called out to Shaffa, "Hey!"

Shaffa, upon hearing my shout, set the container down, turned around, and looked in my direction. "The gate's closed; can you open it so that I can get out?" I asked.

"Sure, Third One!" Shaffa replied. I saw her jog towards the office and go inside to open the gate electronically. Using the rearview mirror, I looked behind me and saw that the gate was opening. I waited until it was fully opened, then I reversed the car out of the warehouse and sped away to company headquarters. I hoped that Face's leg wound would be treated, and I hoped that Jassim's minor injuries would also be mended. But what would happen after that? I supposed that Jassim would be sent to jail after his medical treatment, but what about Face? What would happen to him now? Would he go to prison too?

I mentally shoved those thoughts out of my head and concentrated on driving away.

Headquarters

Due to the heavy midday rush hour traffic, it took me a while to get to the company headquarters. But eventually, through patience and much-welcomed funny conversations with Chibi, I managed to arrive at the place without much hassle.

I deliberately parked my car in the space next to the handicap parking space in order to avoid the risk of a parking fine. I did not wish to take the same risks as the rest of the company members. Taking a risk of this kind was simply was not my way of doing things, and besides, it was not the right time to take such chances.

After switching off the engine, I got out of the car and opened the passenger's side door for Chibi. She hopped out of the car and stood by my side. "Come on Third, let's find Helen!" Chibi said excitedly.

"I'm sure she's at the reception desk, like always," I told Chibi.

"Um...actually, I don't think so," said Chibi. "It's lunch time now, so she will be in her room eating lunch."

I replied, "Okay, then show me where her room is. Lead the way!" With my right hand, I gestured for her to lead me so I could follow her. Chibi pushed the entrance door open, and we both walked inside the building.

As Chibi had confirmed earlier, Helen was not sitting at the reception desk in the lobby. Chibi ran to the elevator door, jumped to push the elevator button, and landed softly on her two plush feet. The elevator door opened, and she hurried inside. I followed her inside and stood still as the elevator door closed. We both waited inside the elevator as it ascended us to the second floor.

*****

Once the elevator door opened on the second floor, where all the office rooms (including my own) were located, I let Chibi get out first so that she could lead me to Helen's room. She walked over to the office door marked with a number four. With her tiny cotton fist she knocked on the door three times, surprising making loud knocking sounds as if her fist was made of either wood or a lightweight metal. Then Chibi yelled, "Hey Helen! It's me, Chibi!"

The door opened for us to enter. I followed Chibi inside, and was amazed at what I saw. Helen's room was very vast and rectangular-shaped in comparison to mine, and contained many flowers all around! The flowers were not in pots or vases, but in square-shaped beds of dark-brown soil. Green vines crept all over the high ceiling, draped on the various ceiling lights hanging overhead. A human-sized sakura tree rested in a large square bed of soil at the far end of the gigantic room, its leaves a vivid pink color. Helen's room looked more like an indoor garden than an office!

So how were the flowers able to grow without sunlight? I wondered. The room was completely walled and without a single window in sight. Additionally, there were only ordinary ceiling lights in the room, not special greenhouse lights that mimic sunlight. Even with these limitations present, all the flowers seemed to be very healthy, with not a single flower wilting. They all gave off a sweet aroma similar to that of women's perfume.

"Helen!" Chibi called out again. "Wake up! It's me, Chibi! Third One is here with me too; we both have a lot to tell you!"

Suddenly, the sakura tree started to change its shape. The leaves all gathered closer together, their color changing from pink to a yellowish tone. The branches also gradually joined up, except for two upper branches of equal length that remained in their places, horizontally from each other, with only the main tree stem separating the two branches. The stump of the tree pulled itself out of the soil, and divided itself into two parts that resembled an upside-down letter 'V'.

I stared in astonishment as the tree transformed itself. What an amazing sight to behold!

I took my eyes off of the tree when I noticed Chibi suddenly scurrying a few feet away from me. She picked up a stray blue-colored cloth that lay on the ground, and tossed it to me. I caught it with both hands, looking at her questioningly. "Third One, cover your eyes with the cloth!" Chibi exclaimed. "That tree over there is Helen; she's changing back into a human. Cover your eyes, fast!"

I immediately understood why Chibi wanted me to cover my eyes. She did not want me to see Helen changing back into human form, since she would presumably be unclothed at the end of the transformation. I obediently covered my eyes and pressed the cloth on my eyelids until I could see nothing but a black darkness. I could only hear the light crackling sounds of wood morphing into flesh-and-blood form. After a while of standing in my spot covering my eyes, I heard a familiar woman's voice, "Chibi, you should have let me know beforehand that someone was with you. I'll go to the bathroom now to get dressed." I heard a door somewhere in the room open, then close. That was my cue to open my eyes again.

I removed the cloth from my face and opened my eyes. I noticed that the sakura tree was not there anymore. I looked around and noticed a door at the left side of the room; I assumed that was the bathroom where Helen had gone to dress up. Chibi stood by my right side, patiently waiting for Helen to come out of the bathroom. Within a few minutes, she came out, dressed in her usual business outfit. "I'm sorry, Mister Third One," Helen apologized, blushing and smiling. "I ate lunch early and decided to take a nap. Chibi did not tell me that you were with her, so I wasn't ready for any guests."

I smiled but I did not say anything. There was an awkward silence for a few seconds. Then I spoke up finally, asking Helen, "So, your special attribute is transforming into a tree...?"

Helen replied, "Yes, although my power isn't really of much use in the company. Just like with Chibi's attributes, I have no idea how I acquired mine. But I truly hope one day I can find out how we both gained our powers."

"Helen told me everything about my past!" Chibi broke in, surprisingly in a happy tone of voice. But I thought Helen did not want to tell Chibi about her past. I thought Helen was afraid that telling her about it would make her sad.

"Yes, that's right," Helen said. "After Chibi was punished following Doctor Six's departure from the company, I decided to reveal her past to her directly. And after telling her the whole story, I did not feel well." Helen took a deep breath, and then continued, "I felt terrible because I had broken my promise. In the end, I felt it was better for Chibi to know about her past. That was why I was not acting like myself the last time we talked, Third One."

"But Helen, I'm *glad* that you told me about my story!" Chibi interjected. "I always wondered why I wasn't a human girl, and after you told me everything, I was *so* happy! You shouldn't feel bad about telling me my past!"

Chibi ran up to Helen and hugged her leg. Helen crouched down, patted Chibi's head, and told her, "I don't feel bad about it anymore, Chibi."

Then I remembered the purpose of me and Chibi coming here. "By the way, Helen," I began, "we actually came here to tell you that a big problem occurred earlier today, during my third mission."

Helen stood up. She listened carefully as Chibi and I explained everything to her.

*****

After we finished talking, Helen stood silently for some seconds. She bit her lower lip, appearing as if she was going to break down in tears. She slowly crouched down and sat on the carpeted floor next to the nearest square-shaped flowerbed. "I – I can't believe th…this is happening…" Helen stammered, her whole body shaking nervously. "I can't…believe it…"

"You'd better believe it," I told Helen, "this company is in danger of extinction as a result of the effects of the mist.

But Shaffa told us not to do anything drastic until she gets here. So we'll have to wait until she shows up."

Helen nodded, and then said bleakly, "So this company building of ours must also be burned down in order to eliminate the evil mist particles."

"It looks like that's the only thing we can do right now. But we should wait for Shaffa to come here so that we can plan everything out properly."

Everyone agreed, and so we all sat down on the floor and waited in Helen's flowery room, chatting about random things until Shaffa arrives. We talked for maybe five to ten minutes, when suddenly we heard someone knocking on the door.

"Wow, Shaffa got back pretty early," I said. Helen got up to go answer the door, but I insisted, "I'll open the door." Helen nodded and allowed me to open it.

After opening the door, I gasped and widened my eyes. The person standing in front of the door was not Shaffa. It was Isaac Warren, the man formerly known as Doctor Six!

Reunion

I stood stunned as the man named Isaac Warren smiled and extended his right hand to shake mine. "Hello there, Third One!" he greeted, his smile broadening. "It's really nice to see you again!"

I slowly and involuntarily extended my right hand, and he took my hand and shook it so hard that I almost lost my balance. Then he gently pulled me close and hugged me.

"Doctor Six!" Chibi hollered merrily, freely calling him by his former name. I looked back and saw her dart towards our direction, her little feet moving so fast that they looked like a blur as she ran. The man let go of me and held his arms out for Chibi, who promptly jumped into his arms like a happy puppy. "I missed you so much!" Chibi cried happily, while hugging Isaac's chest. Helen had a great smile on her face; she obviously missed him as well.

"How did you get out of jail?" Chibi asked him.

"I was never in prison in the first place," Isaac said, while kneeling to lower Chibi down to the floor. "The person who was imprisoned was a decoy, created by yours truly."

I narrowed my eyes at him. "What do you mean by 'created'?" I asked curiously.

Isaac smiled and explained, "For years, I was working on building a humanoid robot in my laboratory, a robot that looked and thought exactly like me from head to toe, with the mechanical parts of the robot deeply hidden inside the artificial flesh, functioning as bones and nerves. I finished building it last year, and I kept it concealed in my lab until I really needed to use it. And sure enough, after Face fired me from working in the company, I went back to my lab located in a remote part of the city, and programmed it to go to the police station to get itself arrested instead of me.

"And while the robot was in prison, I took a taxi to an isolated part of the desert and hid out in the company's emergency shack. This shack is so far away in the desert that even Face himself had forgotten its existence, and the only other person who actually used it before was Shaffa, on one of her early missions in the company."

Upon listening to Isaac's explanation about his doppelganger robot, I immediately thought about Shaffa, who herself was a humanoid robot. "Doctor Six," I began. "We found out that Shaffa is actually a—"

"Robot," Isaac interjected, grinning. "More specifically, a Humanoid Experimental Robot; or HER in short form. Yes, I am fully aware of her background, Third One. I had discovered this fact some time ago."

I pursed my lips. Well since Isaac *is* the company doctor, I should not be surprised that he observed Shaffa long enough to inevitably determine and study her background, I thought.

He suddenly walked past us to look around in Helen's flowery room, observing the surroundings. After about twenty seconds of silent observation of her room, Isaac remarked, "Beautiful room, Miss Helen."

Helen blushed visibly at his compliment and said, "Thank you, Isaac."

He walked back to us and continued, "And so I stayed in the shack, communicating only with Shaffa via mobile phone. She already filled me in on the situation about Face, about how a mysterious 'evil' mist affected him recently and caused him to behave abnormally. Before arriving here, Shaffa informed me that she already explained everything about the evil mist to you, Third One."

I nodded and said, "Yes, and earlier I explained it all to Chibi and Helen." So Shaffa had told Isaac Warren about the mist, and they were cooperating to solve the problem this whole time! Why didn't Shaffa tell me that Isaac was also helping us out?

Shaffa...I seriously don't think I will ever fully understand her!

"Great!" Isaac exclaimed. "Now all we have to do is remain here until Shaffa arrives."

"Uh...doctor?" Chibi uttered softly, raising her hand like a schoolgirl in a classroom.

"What is it, Chibi?"

"What about that poor robot you made, the one that looks like you?" Chibi asked Isaac. "Will he stay in jail forever?"

Isaac paused, then with a solemn expression replied, "I'm afraid so. I made that robot for use in case of an emergency, and Face dismissing me from the company was reason enough for me to use it. I made it as a decoy to prevent me from getting arrested by the police. The police will never know that it is actually a robot, because I engineered the metal parts inside of it in such a way that it will never be detected by metal detectors. It's almost perfectly human in every way, but at the same time it isn't human."

Isaac stepped over to her, crouched down, and gave her a hug. "So don't be sad that it's staying in jail, Chibi. That's basically its job, and it will carry on doing its job for as long as it takes," he told her.

Chibi began to cry. "Don't worry, Chibi. Don't worry about a thing," Isaac said soothingly.

After some moments of Chibi crying like a baby in Isaac's arms, Isaac stood up again and said, "And by the way, my name is not Isaac Warren anymore."

He pulled out a glass vial containing a clear liquid, poured the liquid into the palm of his gloved hand, and smeared the liquid all over his face. I saw the paint on his face rapidly dissolve away, revealing his true normal face. "I programmed the robot to accept its name as 'Isaac Warren', so its name is now Isaac Warren. My name, on the other hand, is Doctor Six. That's the name I proudly want to keep, even though it's not my original birth name, and even though I am no longer officially with the company anymore. As far as I'm concerned, the man named Isaac Warren is now in prison, but the man named Doctor Six is, and will always be, a free man."

Chibi cried even more at Doctor Six's emotional speech and jumped up to cling on him and hug him. Helen smiled, with tears visibly brimming in her eyes. I stood smiling, trying to appear calmly unaffected by the doctor's speech, but truth be told, deep inside I was also emotionally struck by his words. I just decided not to show it.

Now that Doctor Six had no paint on his face, he looked like a normal scientist and not a character from a comic book. The only abnormal features remaining on his face, which were permanent and therefore could not be removed or changed, were his fully white eyes that were without visible pupils or irises. From what I had observed, it seemed that the doctor finally decided to be his true self from now on, rather than someone else. I had absolutely no problem with his decision.

The emotional moment in Helen's room was stopped short when we heard a knock at the door.

I immediately walked over to the door and opened it, much to the surprise of everybody in the room. Shaffa was the one who knocked on the door this time. She smiled when she saw me, the usual robotic smile that she almost always had on her face.

"Hello, Third One!" Shaffa exclaimed contentedly. "I expected that you would be in Helen's room, but I didn't predict that you would be the one to answer the door. Your confidence levels are increasing, and that's a good thing."

What she had just told me after greeting me was weird; I couldn't figure out if she had just told me some kind of a joke or a serious statement. She suddenly gripped my right hand and shook it in salutation. Then she noticed the others behind me and walked over to them.

"Hello, Doctor Six! It's great to see you back in the headquarters again," Shaffa said to the doctor. They both shook hands and said a few more words of greetings. Then Shaffa greeted Helen and commented, "You have a nice room, Helen. It matches you perfectly."

Helen suddenly laughed and said, "Thanks for the compliment, Shaffa."

"You are welcome," Shaffa replied. Chibi pulled on the leg part of Shaffa's jeans, trying to gain her attention. "And what about *me*, Shaffa?" Chibi demanded shrilly.

Shaffa looked down and chuckled. "Oh yes, how could I ever forget about you, Chibi?" She picked her up and hugged her, then set her back down again. Chibi's frowned mouth turned into a smile.

"Alright everyone," Shaffa began in a more serious tone of voice. "We must burn down this building tomorrow morning. Earlier today, I had burned down a company warehouse and destroyed the evil mist particles that were present inside. Our main building must also be burned down in order to destroy the mist particles. I know it is sad that we will not be living here anymore, but burning the place down is the only way to completely get rid of the mist and save us from turning evil.

"Between now and tonight, you all have to pack up your belongings and put them outside your rooms, so that they may be collected by our reinforcements and transported to another building. The reinforcements are waiting outside right now, disguised as movers, to avoid attracting any unwanted attention. In an hour, they will be in the building to gather your luggage and other useful items from the other facilities, and then carry them downstairs to put them in the truck parking outside. You all have plenty of time, so pack everything up. Then after that, get some sleep for the night. We will all leave tomorrow morning at around eight o'clock, so set your alarms."

"But who exactly will burn the company building?" I asked.

"I ordered some of the reinforcements to do that job," Shaffa responded. "Right after we leave this place tomorrow morning, they will set the building on fire and then they will all evacuate the area, leaving the burning building for the local fire department to extinguish. The spare company building we will go to is close to the desert, far enough away from the presence of the mist particles."

"And what about our manager, Face?" Helen asked. "Will he be all right?"

Shaffa said, "The doctors at the hospital said that his injuries should heal up by noon tomorrow, so he should be okay. The mist particles rooted in his body should disappear by tomorrow, since he's not in a place infested with the mist anymore. Any other questions?"

We all shook our heads in unison. "Good," Shaffa said finally. "Now go pack up your things before you all go to sleep tonight."

We all exited the room except for Helen, and headed out to our rooms to pack up our belongings. I looked back and saw Helen's door closing automatically, catching a glimpse of her walking back to the spot that I saw her at when she was in her tree form.

How was she going to pack up all her flowers? I thought. Perhaps Shaffa would solve that problem. After all, she greatly helped in solving most of the problems that happened today. I assumed that Shaffa would be able to figure out how Helen's flowers can be properly transported.

Once I got back to my office room, I packed all my belongings into the cardboard box that was still in my room, taped it shut using duct tape that I found in my desk drawer, set the box outside of my room next to the door, ate a quick dinner, and then I went to sleep.

Moving

We all left the company headquarters at seven o'clock, an hour earlier than the scheduled timing. According to Shaffa, all the belongings and supplies in the HQ were put into a semi-truck by the time the morning sun rose in the sky. The semi-truck that was parked outside the building was spacious enough to hold and transport everything we needed from the building. However, a great many things were left behind, which included items such as furniture, technology, and chemicals. Only those few furniture, technology, and chemical items that we really needed were transported; all other items that fell out of the 'useful' category were left behind.

That morning was the first time I had ever seen so many company members gathered together; there were at least thirty uniformed employees helping to carry the company possessions from the building to the truck's cargo area, resembling the way ants carry food crumbs to their nest. All the company reinforcements helping with the big move wore uniforms, in order to avoid attracting unwanted attention of passing civilians and local authority figures. The reinforcements, as Shaffa explained to me that morning, functioned as both the 'helping hands' and the 'backup forces' of the company. They were stationed in various places in different parts of the world in case they were ever needed in times of emergencies.

Once the luggage and goods (and Helen's flowers included) were safely stowed away inside the box trailer of the semi-truck, we all drove away from the vicinity of the building so that the reinforcements staying behind would be able to properly set the building on fire. Shaffa led the way at the front, driving the beat-up gray van that Doctor Six had driven during my first mission with the company, with Doctor Six and Helen riding along with her. The semi-truck followed the van, and I drove carefully in my own car behind the truck, with Chibi riding with me in the passenger's seat. The trip to the spare company building took about an hour due to the morning traffic, but I was not at all troubled. I passed the time away by talking and laughing with Chibi about random things.

We eventually turned off the highway and into a dirt road that led to the open desert, passing a big yellow signboard along the way that read 'Private Road' in large font letters. The dirt road was smooth enough for all our vehicles to get through; it was properly shaped in a way that suited even the wheels of a small compact car, so there was no worry of any of our vehicles getting stuck in the sand. I assumed the company reinforcements maintained this dirt road on a regular basis to make sure it stayed accessible at all times for all the company's land vehicles.

The truck in front of me slowed down and halted to a stop, so I pressed the brake to stop as well. I wanted to see why everyone stopped in front of me, but the semi truck's massive box trailer blocked my line of vision. Chibi, obviously noticing the look of uneasiness on my face, said in her high-pitched voice, "Don't worry, Third One, we're very close to the spare building! Shaffa will make the gate open for us to drive in!"

I looked to Chibi, smiling at her in relief. After a few seconds, I noticed the truck in front of me accelerated forward, so I also started moving ahead. When I finally reached the gate, which was now opened, I saw two uniformed gatekeepers waving their hands at me. I waved back to them with my right hand, smiling. I noticed that on both sides of the gate were rows upon rows of tall metallic fences that stretched out for miles, so far away that I could not see where the fences had ended. *The company must have spent heaps of money on purchasing this long stretch of land and constructing the fences,* I thought.

Now that I passed the gate, I continued following the truck in front of me, seeing nothing but desert sand and vegetation everywhere, until reaching a point where the environment was totally different from what I expected to see:

There were long rows of palm trees extending as far out as the fences I had seen earlier, with the smooth dirt road now replaced with a light grassy road mixed with gravel. As I rolled along, I passed gardens containing flowers, fruits, and vegetables of all kinds. Various people were walking around, some uniformed and some not, stopping occasionally to look at us. Everyone in this place was smiling in a way that resembled Shaffa's infamous robotic smile.

Then the grassy road turned into asphalt as we drove into a humongous parking area containing many parked cars and trucks. As the semi-truck turned to the right to park somewhere, I saw a very wide rectangular-shaped building up ahead. Since the truck turned away, the van driven by Shaffa was now in plain view ahead of me, picking up speed as it neared the building. I accelerated hard to catch up and my car's engine roared, jetting past the van and towards the empty parking spaces that lay directly in front of the building. I parked in one of the free spaces, switched off the engine of my car, and got out to wait for Shaffa and the others. I opened the door for Chibi and she instantly jumped outside, standing next to me to wait for them.

When Shaffa finally arrived, she parked the van next to my car and exited the vehicle, with the others getting out after her. Shaffa walked up to me and laughed. "Ah yes, Third One, you won the race!" she joked. Chibi then said, "Yeah, of course! Third One's car is way faster than that junky van! We should make all our company cars as fast as Third One's car!" Doctor Six winked and gave me a thumbs-up, and Helen smiled at me.

"Okay everyone," Shaffa started, "go inside and let the company reinforcements escort you to your temporary rooms. I will go back to the city and pick up Face from the hospital."

"But what about our stuff from the truck?" Chibi demanded.

"All your things will have to be kept in the truck for now," Shaffa replied, "as I do not know how long we will be staying here to work. Only our manager Face has the authority to decide on that, so please be patient until I bring him here."

We all nodded, but Chibi only nodded lightly, her facial expression neutral and unsmiling. I assumed that she still didn't get over what Face had put her through when he punished her and attempted to execute her, whilst he was under the influence of the evil mist. Under the circumstances,

Chibi's reluctance to see Face again was understandable. I hoped that Chibi would forgive Face after he apologizes to everyone for his actions, because it was not Face's fault that he acted evil. The mysterious 'evil' company, and the 'evil' mist that its employees sprayed, should be wholly blamed for the evil things that Face had done.

Shaffa walked away from us to a white-colored sports utility vehicle that was parked nearby. She took a key out of her pocket to unlock the car, then hopped in and started the engine. After she reversed out of the parking space and drove away, we all walked into the front entrance of the building, side by side.

We were greeted by smiling young men and women in blue uniforms that resembled those of a police force, all with conspicuous badges bearing the company name, and their own names imprinted in bright white color on their breast pockets. The majestic lobby was filled with white and yellow lights shining from various chandeliers, and fancy-looking furniture and technological devices lined the walls. Several wall-mounted televisions were displaying different news channels as some employees stood watching them from the screens, while others used tablets mounted on water fountain-like pedestals to surf the internet. A long reception desk lay at the end of the room, with several elevator doors on either side of it. Three receptionists sat behind the desk, smiling at us.

"Please, follow us," said one of the uniformed people who greeted us. She and three others gestured for us all to follow them. "We will show you to your rooms."

We all followed them to one of the elevator doors at the right of the reception desk. The elevator button was pushed by the woman in uniform who earlier spoke up, and the door immediately opened. The interior space of the elevator was astonishingly big enough for as many as thirty people!

Everyone entered the roomy elevator before its door closed. The walls of the elevator were lined with magnificent paintings, all of which were very captivating to look at. For example, one painting depicted a gigantic palm tree in the middle of a city that grew so tall its leaves hovered over the buildings. Another painting showed a stream of water flowing from a river into a jug, the river's vast width decreasing as it got closer to the jug. These paintings, along with the other ones next to and around them, look as if they should have been displayed on the walls of an art museum rather than the interior walls of an elevator!

After a minute of waiting in the elevator and observing the paintings, the elevator finally stopped and its doors opened. The company members in uniform led us out of the elevator and into a hallway that greatly resembled the hotel-esque hallway on the second floor of our former headquarters, except that this particular hall was much wider and had more doors.

We were given the keys to our rooms. After the uniformed company members bid us farewell and went back into the elevator, we all entered our rooms. Helen went into her room first, and then Doctor Six, then Chibi, then me.

My room looked exactly like a hotel bedroom, which was no surprise to me, considering that the hallway already looked like that of a hotel. A king-sized bed, a table, and a miniature refrigerator sat on the red-carpeted floor at the right wall of the room. A door to the bathroom was to the left, and a dresser and a closet lay next to the door. At the straight end of the room, a dark red curtain concealed a big window. I opened the curtains and looked outside. I saw a long stretch of desert, extending as far as my eyes could see. Not much of an interesting view, I thought, but at least it was a peaceful sight compared to the hustle-and-bustle of the city life that I had lived before. I was glad that there were still places like this in existence, where one can bask in tranquility and take a break from the fast-paced nature of the city.

I plopped myself on the bed and closed my eyes, allowing myself to fall asleep. I decided to sleep for a while because I was feeling very tired from the long trip to the building. I had forgotten to set an alarm before sleeping, but that was okay. One of my fellow colleagues was bound to wake me up whenever Shaffa came back from the hospital with Face.

Gathering

And sure enough, someone woke me up from sleep. "Third One?" a familiar man's voice called from behind my door, accompanied by the sounds of a hand knocking on it. It was Doctor Six.

I stretched out my arms and yawned, and got out of bed. I opened my door and saw him standing there. "Shaffa has just arrived with Face," said Doctor Six. "Come on, let's go and meet them."

I followed the doctor into the open elevator, and stood still as the elevator door closed. Once again, I was surrounded by the wonderful paintings; I observed them once again before the elevator reached its destination. Then its door opened. "Come on, Third One," Doctor Six ordered. I stepped outside the elevator with him.

We walked into what looked like an enormous conference room, complete with several meeting tables and chairs. A wall-sized glass window was at the end of this huge room, wholly revealing the view of the desert land outside. Shaffa, Helen, and Chibi were sitting next to each other at one of the tables, with Face sitting at the far end. Doctor Six and I walked over to the table and took our seats. He sat next to Chibi, and I sat next to him.

Face looked somewhat different from before. He wore his typical outfit, but the skin on his face looked a lot less pale than usual, making him look more human and less ghostly.

"Hello there, Third One!" Face greeted happily. "I deeply apologize for my erratic behavior last week." I smiled cautiously at him, and then he stood up and began his speech:

"During the drive here, Shaffa explained everything to me. She also informed me of the reasons why I was acting strangely. At first, I didn't believe her because I was apparently too far affected by the evil mist to listen to reason. Now that I'm in a place where there is no trace of the mist, I am able to think clearly again. I realized that I had done very wrong things last week, and I take back every single wrong word I said to all of you. In short, no one sitting in this room is fired from his or her job; despite what I had said while I was under the influence of the mist, you are all still employees of this marvelous company of ours. Everyone, please forgive me for my terrible words and actions last week and every week before that. Please disregard any evil statement I made or any evil action I did before. Now that I am cured from the effects of the mist, I promise you that will never again be influenced by evil ever again. I will continue to be a good person, and I strongly hope you all remain good people. Thank you."

We all clapped our hands after Face finished his speech and sat back down on his seat. Face smiled but lowered his head, the brim of his fedora hat covering his sad eyes. At first I thought Face was going to cry, but then he lifted his head and stood up again from his seat. "Doctor Six, please come here," Face ordered with a smile. The doctor obediently got up from his chair and went up to him. Face extended his right hand. "I am very sorry for everything, Doctor," Face apologized. Doctor Six shook Face's hand, and then responded, "Don't worry about it, Face. It wasn't your fault, after all. That evil company was to blame for everything." Face gave the doctor a quick hug, and then allowed him to go back to his seat.

Face then sat back down and said, "And Chibi, I greatly apologize for what I had put you through. I hope you can forgive me for everything, even though the things I did would have led to the end of your life."

Chibi hopped onto the table, ran to Face, and hugged him. "Don't worry, Face," Chibi uttered tearfully, "I'm not mad at you anymore, and I'm sorry for screaming at you and calling you a monster that time. I'm glad that you are back to normal, because I didn't like it when you were acting evil. I forgive you!"

Face patted Chibi on her head, saying, "Thanks for accepting my apology, Chibi. I promise you that I will never act evil ever again."

Chibi then let go of Face and sat down in front of him on the table, facing us. Her cottony face was all moist with happy tears and a cheerful expression.

"And you Third One," Face said, "please come here."

I got up and walked over to where Face was sitting. Face immediately got up and hugged me, then he let go and said, "I am very sorry for how I treated you yesterday. As you already know, I was so heavily influenced by the effects of the mist particles embedded within me that I wasn't aware of the wrongs I was doing. I feel especially terrible that I had acted evilly towards you, since you are currently the newest member of the company. Please forgive me and forget about the evil things that I had said and done."

I smiled and simply replied to him, "I forgive you for everything."

"That's good to hear, Third One," Face commented. I walked back to my chair and sat down. "And I ask you too, Shaffa, to forgive me for the way I treated you. I didn't mean to underestimate you and the special talents that you have. Without your help and intervention, this company would have been destroyed. I honor you for not being afraid to take action yesterday."

Shaffa remained seated but smiled and said, "I forgive you, and thanks for honoring me."

"You're welcome," Face said. Then he looked at Helen and asserted, "I don't recall doing anything evil to you, Helen, but—"

"It's all right, Face, I forgive you for your actions," Helen quickly divulged, smiling. "I could not possibly reject your apologies after everyone accepted them. And besides, as Doctor Six mentioned, you are not to blame for all that you had done."

"Thank you, Miss Helen," Face said. Then he stated, "I would also like to mention something else: Keith, Greg, and the gang leader Jassim, the three people whom I had wrongly hired into the company, are now in prison where they belong. Never again will I accept such kinds of people to be employed into this good company of ours."

"So where are we going to live now?" Chibi asked in her shrill mousy voice.

Face patted her head again and said, "Well, since our main building is now gone, we will have to go to another one of our main buildings in another country."

The room fell silent for a few seconds. Then Chibi broke the silence by asking, "Why can't we just stay working here in this building?"

"Because this building is reserved only for our reinforcements," Face answered smartly. "Also, this building, as big as it already is, would not have enough room for all our equipment from our old H.Q. And we cannot afford to waste time building a new compound to replace the previous main building, so it's best to travel to another country and work in a ready-made H.Q."

"But what about this country?" I demanded. "Who is going to be responsible for promoting good and stopping evil here if we leave?"

"Why, our reinforcements, of course," Face responded casually. "They are stationed everywhere here. Now that they are aware of the evil company's activities, they will be extra vigilant in combating evil. But you must understand, Third One, that the citizens and authority figures in the country are perfectly capable of encouraging good and preventing evil on their own. It is not always necessary for our reinforcements to keep an eye on things here, because the people living in the country can take responsibility for their own actions. The reinforcements are only there to deal with the bigger problems."

Face was right. The people living in my home country had their own moral standards, and they lived by those standards as much as they could. They can handle problems on their own, and they did not really need any outside help to give them advice on what is right and wrong; they already know what is right and wrong. But of course, some people in the country, for whatever reasons, get tempted to do wrong instead of right, therefore causing crime and conflict. This phenomenon happens in every single country across the globe, sometimes on a smaller scale and sometimes on a larger scale.

Everyone makes mistakes and nobody is perfect; it is only a matter of choosing between right and wrong. And that choice is up to the people to make, for themselves and for the society around them.

"So which country will we travel to?" I asked Face.

He answered, "We will be travelling to Rome, the capital of Italy. The company headquarters building located there had just been built a few months ago, and it is newly furnished and ready for use, with plenty of space for our equipment from the previous headquarters. Tonight, I'll arrange for a plane to take us there at the end of this week. In the meantime, I have a small mission for you, Third One."

Face walked up to me, took out a piece of folded yellow paper from his trench coat pocket, and handed it to me. I unfolded the paper and looked at it. It was a map.

"Tomorrow night," Face began, "I would like you to go to the area shown in the map. It is the area where the company's emergency shack is located, the one where Doctor Six was hiding out after he was falsely dismissed from the company. Today I will have reinforcements go over there and make preparations for your mission."

I looked at Face quizzically. "So, this mission is going to be staged?" I asked him.

He then replied, "Yes, Third One, this mission will be a staged mission. Consider this particular mission to be a test. I want you to go to the company shack and write about all that has happened. After reading the reports you had previously given me, I can see that your writing skills are excellent. I would like you to use those skills of yours to write a book about everything that happened so far, exclusively from your own point of view."

"B-but," I stammered nervously, still surprised about the description of this mission, "from where should I begin the story?"

"Start at any point in your life, in any way you want," Face said. "And after you're done, one of my associates here will collect the book from you and bring it to me. Then once we get to Rome, I will publish your book to the world so that readers from everywhere can know that our company exists. The reason why I want the story written by you is because you are the only employee in this company who has a heart full of good and truth. You were never affected by the mist, and for that reason I know that you would write the story in the most honest manner possible.

"And once someone arrives to collect your book, you will be told hints to the whereabouts of a very special thing hidden somewhere near the shack. Think of this next assignment within the mission as an easy treasure hunt; you will be rewarded with the special thing that you will find.

"Also, about the writing half of your mission, I will have enough writing material delivered to the shack, so don't worry about running out of paper or ink."

I carefully took in all of what he said, memorizing his instructions. I was confident enough to carry out this mission, even though at first I was nervous about it. After all that has happened in my life so far since graduation from university, I was now willing to tell the whole world about everything that has happened, no matter how unbelievable everything would appear in the form of words in a book.

"Okay everyone," Face announced, "how about we all have some lunch downstairs in the restaurant area? They've prepared some great food for us today!"

So, after the conclusive sounds of us all happily chattering, we all agreed to go and have lunch. Chibi, Doctor Six, Helen, Shaffa, and I all walked side by side to the door, with Face tagging along behind us. I looked back only to notice Face laughing happily by himself, his laughter showing no signs of evil anymore.

Epilogue

As of this writing, you, my dear reader, have come to the end of the first part of my story. After completing the previous chapter, I slept for the night and waited patiently the next morning for a company member to arrive and pick up the book I had written. And sure enough, as I expected, Shaffa had arrived. She told me to look behind the shack for the 'special thing' (which I had previously mentioned as '*it*') that Face wanted me to find.

So I looked around the back of the shack and saw something red-colored behind an overgrown desert bush. I reached through the bush with both my hands, successfully pulling out the object that was behind the bush leaning against the shack. It was a medium-sized red cardboard box. I opened the box and saw a golden trophy laying on its side, with engravings at the front. I took out the trophy by its two side handles and examined it. A piece of paper holding a message was taped to the front, right below the fancy engravings. I carefully peeled the paper off the trophy surface and read the message written on it:

This trophy is exclusively awarded to you, Third One, for your bravery in the face of evil and your confidence in

resisting evil. You are truly the one who has the will to continue the legacy of the late previous member named as 'The Third One.' You have an equally good heart and soul, good enough to keep this company alive and strong enough to resist evil.

Thank you so much for your great efforts in our company, Third One. I hope you gain even more blessings full of goodness in your life while working in the company.

Your friend and manager,
Face

I looked behind the paper and found the following written:

Chibi wants to sit next to you on the flight to Rome.

I chuckled and felt a rush of happiness inside of me. I knew that the golden trophy Face had given to me was *it*, the special thing, but the words written on this piece of paper felt far more special than the trophy itself. I folded the paper carefully and put it into my pocket, making a promise to keep this paper with me forever. I couldn't wait to meet my fellow colleagues again, and travel with them to Rome. I was very happy about travelling there, because it meant that I would be getting closer to where my family lived. Perhaps one day I would be able to see them again. Hopefully, Face would allow me to someday travel to America to visit them.

I carried the trophy with me back to the shack and saw that Shaffa was still in there. She had asked me if there was anything else I wanted to write down before collecting the book from me, so I wrote this:

I am sure that my story will be categorized as a work of fiction due to its seemingly unrealistic contents, but that does not bother me at all. It is up to you, my dear reader, to decide for yourself whether my story was real or not.

You are free to think of my story however you want to think of it, but remember that my story does not really end here. My story is far from over, and it only goes on further as the battle between good and evil in my life continues.

END